THE GLENNMARE GIRLS

A novel

ANYA MORA

JOFFE BOOKS

Joffe Books, London
www.joffebooks.com

First published in Great Britain in 2023

Cover art by Imogen Buchanan

ISBN: 978-1-83526-307-5

CHAPTER 1. FREDDY

The ferry was a downright disaster. Late, due to fog. Every day, the boat moves across the same stretch of water on the hour, every hour, yet the weather keeps us from getting there in a timely manner.

I'm finally on the island — the great island Wells loves for some ungodly reason. I mean, for chrissakes, it's in the middle of nowhere. The few times we spoke after he moved out west — before he began only responding to letters — he sounded less and less like himself. More and more like a ghost. Like the Wells I met freshman year at Yale. When he was still stuck in his horrific past and hadn't yet learned to live with the elite.

He moved to this wilderness to get himself turned around.

Now, he's more lost than ever. It's his memories that are missing, though, not his mind. Thank God for that. Wells is a brilliant asshole who, for a long time, made my life bearable just by being in it. Tippy's too.

My phone buzzes and I move to answer it, one hand on the wheel of the rental car, the other finding speakerphone. "Hello?"

"Freddy? Where are you?"

Tippy. My heart both constricts and expands.

"Nearly there." I'm searching for a street sign. Finding instead a private road with signage for Glennmare Academy on the left, I turn. "Coming onto the property now," I say, but the call is dropped, Tippy is gone and I am left alone, in the dark.

I flick the bright headlights on, and the pavement beneath the vehicle is finally visible. It's dark, nearly nine at night, but the large expanse of the academy is before me, at the end of a long, tree-lined driveway. The silhouette of Glennmare is one of the reasons wealthy parents send their daughters here. It's impressive, even to me, a man who grew up in Manhattan, with its skyline that people dream of all their lives.

Glennmare is an estate you would expect to find in the English countryside. But it was never owned by a duke or a lord. Instead, it was designed and built by Henry Ellis, a steel tycoon who came into his fortune before the Great Depression. After he died, the property was purchased by a minted Luddite couple who had the idea of creating a school for young girls to learn and explore nature, without modernity getting in the way. Over time the school became more prestigious as the finest teachers were hired. Soon unruly daughters of affluent East Coast families were exiled to the island.

At least, this is what the Wikipedia page told me. I read up on this place while waiting at JFK, wishing that Tippy and I could fly here together. I was in Manhattan when we got word of Wells' fall. She was at a writers' retreat on the windy shores of Oregon, where she was working on her novel.

She's been working on her novel for years, and I don't think she is past the third chapter. But I never comment on it; it is her project and I love her despite the many reasons I cannot stand her. She has been my best friend since we were sixteen.

She is also my stepsister.

I drive past the large, looming academy, beyond the horse stables, and park in front of a tidy row of half-a-dozen cobblestone cottages. After getting out of the car, I reach for my luggage in the trunk. Porch lights illuminate each cottage and I look for his address: *Hollyhock*. All of them are named after indigenous flowers.

This has been Wells' home for the last six months.

I can't help but fear what he remembers.

CHAPTER 2. WELLS

I would tell you my story if I could remember it.

I've been told that yesterday I fell off a horse. I woke in a hospital bed with no memories of the last six months. Now back home, in a cottage I can't remember moving into, I am trying to piece my world together.

"Wells, are you even listening?" Tippy's voice is tight, her eyes like the sea, dark blue enough to drown in. She holds a pill bottle and a glass of water. My bedroom is dim, but she is a bright light. Even after everything, I'm grateful she is here.

"I'm listening." I try to appease her. She's flown to be at my bedside and the last thing I want is to hurt her more than I already have.

"Freddy is on his way," she says, handing me the medicine. "He's quite upset."

"With me?" I sit up, instantly regretting it. Ribs broken, mind shattered. Everything hurts. Without my recent memories I am nothing but a shell. Who am I now?

"You? God, no. Here, drink this." She presses the glass into my hand, waits for me to sip, and then sits on the bed, her hand cupping my cheek. "Freddy is upset because his best friend nearly died and can't remember a thing about the last six months. You never should have moved to this island. It's nothing like home."

"I needed a change; *we* needed a change," I tell her, remembering that bit at least. Everything from before September is clear in my mind. I remember being hired, over the phone, by Duncan Wright, the headmaster at the Glennmare Academy. I remember leaving Connecticut and moving to the rugged terrain that spans the beaches, hills and farmland of Whidbey. An island planted in the deep waters of the Puget Sound, a stretch of land ten miles across and thirty-seven miles long, ninety minutes from Seattle.

It is a beautiful place, but it was the horses at the academy that won me over. The stables are a sentimental nod to my childhood, one I was so removed from for so long. I never wanted to return to my uncle's dusty barn, instead wanting a grander life. Maybe that is where I went wrong. Maybe it is the only place I really belonged. Coming here felt like I was returning to forgotten parts of myself.

Of course, I also chose to accept this teaching position because I needed space from Tippy and Frederick. It was time I carved a life for myself, separate from them. But whatever I've carved here doesn't seem good.

I wish I knew what caused the trouble I'm now in.

Because there *is* trouble.

Tippy has said as much.

The police are waiting to question me. The headmaster has scheduled a meeting. A girl is missing.

And I can't remember anything.

CHAPTER 3. JOHANNA

While I am the cook at this academy, I also pride myself on tidying up after the day's work is done. Dusting, sweeping — anything to let me take full advantage of the quiet. After all, the evening hours, when the girls are all in their rooms for the night, are the perfect time to listen in.

And they need me to listen in, to look after them. There are no mothers here, no one to guide them in this world. And though I wouldn't tell a soul, they are what keep me alive. After losing my daughter, I moved here and lost myself in them, in their lives.

The portrait-lined halls are empty and still, each bed filled with a teenage girl who wears ribbons in her hair, a nod to innocence I am not so naïve as to believe they hold. They are high-school girls, the ones who come here — and they arrive at the island after they have burned bridges elsewhere. Though it isn't a school for troubled girls per se, the ones who arrive on this wind-blown island are trying to run from something. Growing up is hard no matter where you come from. And these girls — all of them — come from money.

Fires blaze beneath the mantels; we need every fire-place lit on a February night like this when the power is out. Everything has been on the fritz the last twenty-four hours and it's all because of him. I know he has something to do with this mess. Not the power going out — he isn't some sort of magician — but I swear to God he has too many of the girls here under his spell.

Now Glennmare is in a tizzy. Of course, Wells Halifax, that young upstart from the mainland, would get himself thrown from a horse, forgetting what he did to get there. And sweet Kitty, still missing.

I blame him, entirely.

I told Duncan it was a terrible misstep, hiring him. A young, smug man from the East Coast with more education than the girls here need in a teacher. His specialty, apparently, is ancient literature. Something more practical would benefit the students. God knows these girls need all the sensible training they can get. Still, I wish my Matilda could have been at a school like this. Everything would have been so different for her. The students here have so much freedom. Not one of them confined to a box, and I do my part to ensure they don't feel trapped.

Despite my reservations — and there were plenty — Duncan hired Wells Halifax in late summer. What kind of twenty-five-year-old man wears second-hand suits? The kind that also smokes cigarettes and quotes from obscure novels during staff meetings to show how clever he is.

Duncan needed Wells to teach, but he also wanted someone for the stables, so he hired him and tacked that on to his job. The girls wanted to ride the horses more, and they needed a supervisor. But if that was the reason for bringing him to Glennmare, why not offer him a job in the stables? Of course, when I asked Duncan this, he told me I was not there to give input, that I was the cook and should stay in the kitchen.

Duncan is sixty-eight and hasn't a clue about how old he sounds. He certainly couldn't get away with talking to a woman that way in the city.

But we aren't in the city. And their laws don't apply at Glennmare.

Ask the girls. They've written their own rule book.

CHAPTER 4. FREDDY

There are deep-purple cabbages in pots on the porch of the cottage to the right. On the left, there is a red bicycle, resting on its kickstand. The only thing to note about Wells' place is the lack of a welcome mat.

I shuffle my feet against the floor of the empty porch, out of habit, then rap my knuckles against the wooden door. Immediately, it swings open.

Tippy stands with eyes fraught with fear. "You scared me."

"Why? You knew I was coming."

"Sure, but it's spooky here, isn't it?"

I step inside the house. The only light comes from the flames in the fireplace, flickering orange and yellow, and a candle that Tippy holds. She transfers it to her left hand as she locks the front door.

"Power is out," she explains. "And the cell service is non-existent, which is why the call dropped."

"I figured. Calls never go through with Wells," I say, exaggerating. Wells and I haven't been speaking, but I don't want her to know the extent of that. "And there's no WiFi on this archaic property. It's why we resorted to letter-writing since he moved."

Tippy smirks. "Forever nostalgic for a simpler time, the two of you." She presses a palm to her cheek, as if remembering something. Me. Him.

I set my bags on the wood-planked floor and survey the room. Clearly, Wells wasn't the one to furnish the space. Too much lace, for one. Crocheted doilies on the edges of the couch and the pair of armchairs, on the center of a small dining table for four, on the top of a piano in the corner. "What the hell is this place?"

Tippy shrugs, turning to the hall. "Cottagecore gone wrong."

"How is he?" I follow her candlelight, pausing when she does, her hand on a door left ajar.

"A mess," she says, softly. "Like he was when we found him."

Her words take me back seven years. We came upon Wells late one night, in the middle of our freshman year, on the steps of Old Campus. He was rolling a cigarette, tears in his eyes, and when we approached him, cautiously, we noticed the Moleskine in his lap, pages scribbled in jet-black ink.

"What's wrong?" Tippy asked him. She wore a pale-pink beret, an emerald-green wool coat to her ankles, black loafers, frilly white socks, wide-legged trousers, and a white collared shirt she stole from me. She also looked young and beautiful, like a nymph from a Shakespearean play. Radiant under the moonlight, her eyes sparkling, cheeks rosy, the world her oyster and she knew it.

He looked at Tippy, wiping his cheeks, then moving to light his cigarette with a match he'd struck. It didn't take. He tried again. Then I leaned close enough, offering him my lighter. The one stolen from my father before we left for Yale. An embarrassing memento considering what a terrible man he is.

And one which tortured me, always having him at my fingertips.

Wanting to strike up a conversation, I asked, "Rough day, is it?"

Wells may have been crying and blathering in an old journal — but it was immediately obvious that he was a man I wanted to know. He had an edge about him that I always lacked, a depth I was yet to find. He was that dark and brooding sort of person who drew you in each time he brushed his hair from his eyes, ran a hand over his neck. He looked like the tortured hero. Like he spent his entire life being a handsome yet misunderstood man.

He offered us cigarettes from the antique case in the pocket of his rumpled, tweed suit coat and we both accepted, sitting beside him. I lit Tippy's, then mine, inhaling as I waited for this stranger to expound.

"This whole place is an illusion and I can hardly bear it," he said with a wry voice I knew well. It was so like my own. I smiled.

"The question, O me! so sad, recurring — What good amid these, O me, O life?" Tippy pursed her lips, eyebrows playfully lifted.

He smiled. "*Answer. That you are here* — that life exists and identity."

Tippy clapped. "Well, now we must be friends forever. Freddy here certainly won't quote Walt Whitman with me."

"It's settled," he said, his eyes on hers. "I'm Wells Halifax, and you are?"

She spoke for herself. "Tippy Brimble."

"Frederick Rooper," I added.

"And the tears?" Tippy pressed. "Is it really so bad here?"

"I grew up in Appalachia. Lived in a trailer with my drunk uncle, parents long gone. Working at a supermarket after school." Wells scoffed. "This place? It's a mirage. Nothing here is real."

"A will-o'-the-wisp?" Tippy asked.

He smiled. "So you understand me. And where do the two of you come from?"

Tippy's cheeks were already red. I took a puff before answering. "Manhattan."

Wells looked us over, then. Tippy's clothes, though disheveled, were all designer. Mine similarly so. A tailored suit, shoes from a department store. My leather satchel bought on a summer trip to the Amalfi Coast.

"The powerful play goes on, and you may contribute a verse." Wells' voice fell flat, though filled with words written decades before by the poet they'd been quoting. He gazed past us, no longer interested in our story.

We forced him to give us a second look.

"Come with us to the party at Union," Tippy said. "We can get drunk and tell the world to fuck off."

Tippy rarely swore, and I knew immediately she wanted Wells to like her. I forced a smile. "You can't sit here and cry. It's not a good look," I said ruefully. "And anyways, we may come from money, but we are absolute misanthropes. We hate everyone who isn't us."

That made him laugh, and he stood, accepting the invitation, recognizing that we were asking him to join our duo, at least for one night. Of course, one night turned into a string of days and weeks and years.

Maybe we saw him as a project, a good deed. An orphan, certainly. But I know it was more than that. Wells Halifax may have resisted us at first, but that was only because he didn't yet know how alike we were, once we stripped away the fact that we had trust funds. And in time, he learned that the money from our family made his life better, too. At least that is what I tell myself.

That day on the steps, Wells was lost. And we found him.

Though, that is merely how I see it. Tippy wants to believe it was he who found her.

Now, as I walk into Wells' bedroom using the light on my phone, I see him sleeping. Tippy stands behind me. The three of us together, again.

Wells has lost the last six months of memories, but I wonder if he wished he could go back in time and never have met Tippy and me at all.

CHAPTER 5. DETECTIVE LEONARD ABBOTT

This prep school where the missing girl was last seen is different from the other island schools. Certainly different from the public high school my daughter, Cassidy, attends. Which happens to be the same one I went to twenty years ago.

The grounds of Glennmare are impressive even if they haven't modernized any of the buildings, as far as the local carpenters and plumbers tell me. Even though I've lived my whole life on this island, locals have no place on this property. Even the cook, Johanna Vestige, moved here for the job. The teachers at the school arrive on ferries, rightfully enamored with the generous salary. The yearly tuition is triple my annual pay.

The case before me now is a tricky one. Katherine Calloway: a missing girl, eighteen years old, gone for thirty hours. She ended up at Glennmare because she kept bolting from her parents' home in Charleston. Fed up with her antics, they sent her to our island.

She's lived here a year, and now she's gone.

I told the police chief, Janice Richards, that Katherine was a runner. But she says it's not so cut and dried. Katherine was an accomplished horse rider and well liked; she had no reason to bolt.

She also had a habit of sneaking off to the gas station and getting an adult to buy her alcohol. We can't trace all the people she would get to buy her booze, but hopefully we can track down a few.

I reviewed the surveillance footage. It was her weekly ritual, and she was always successful.

Now, it's my job to find out what happened. Obtain evidence. Interview witnesses, teachers, her friends.

But to be blunt, I think her parents deserve the truth: their daughter may never come home. At eighteen, she is a legal adult.

I could be wrong — it happens. But I bet Katherine caught a ferry, found a good time in Seattle and doesn't plan on looking back. Chief Richards wants to know how I can be so sure, so I tell her the truth.

When I was in high school, my friends and I would have bonfires on the beach, with beer and pot. Four guys, in the same grade at school, far from popular. We pissed off our parents, stole their liquor and ignored our curfews.

One night a few of those Glennmare girls came out of the woods to join us.

We offered them the escape they craved. Twigs were tangled in their hair; they wore nightgowns but no shoes. Greedy, ready to take, and we gave.

We paired off, over our heads in the way most boys are at sixteen. They knew what they were doing and didn't wait for us to take an awkward lead.

After, they smiled like they had secrets and we fumbled for our pants as they left without looking back.

I grew up, stopped drinking and smoking, found friends my father approved of. But whenever I passed those guys I used to hang out with, in the halls at school, or, later, on the streets of Whidbey, we'd share a knowing look filled with that single memory.

Look, I'm not saying all the girls that go to the academy are easy. I'm just saying twenty-something years ago, one of them sat on my lap without so much as telling me her name and fucked me.

CHAPTER 6. WELLS

The house is quiet when I wake, my side aching, my head foggy. My dream from last night at the edges of my mind, threatening to fade. I close my eyes, trying to hold on to whatever is left of it, and drift back to sleep.

A young woman in a white dress, I try to see her face, but she turns her back to me, her gown falling to the floor. I step closer, I speak. "We shouldn't."

"We must," she whispers.

I startle awake again, gripping the sheets. The house is ice, the pale morning light filtering through the bottom of the curtained bedroom window. *We must.*

Pulling a robe around me, I find my way into the cold kitchen, lighting the gas stove and setting a kettle that came with the house on top of the flame.

Tippy, in a thick cream-colored cable-knit sweater, finds me as I'm adding logs to the fireplace, desperate to warm the freezing cottage.

"You shouldn't be doing this." Her care for me verges on motherly, yet she doesn't look the part of a matron at all. She is as beautiful as she was at eighteen. More so, maybe. The last conversations I remember us having were fueled with anger and jealousy. Now she seems settled, content.

And she's here. Maybe time does heal all wounds. Maybe my accident has turned me into an optimist. Anything would be better than what I was before.

"You need to be resting," she chides. "And let me change your bandages. The doctor said every six hours. It's been seven, at least."

"Did Frederick make it?" I ask, adding kindling, striking a match, tiptoeing around the truth of what we ended. Tippy and me, we went up in flames eight months ago.

"You were already asleep when he got in."

"How did he seem?" I ask, knowing my fall from the horse has caused the two people closest to me to leave their lives without notice. There's nothing I loathe more than being inconvenient, especially to Tippy and Frederick. They've done so much for me already, and I know I haven't exactly returned the favor. This friendship has always been out of balance. Freddy giving and giving, Tippy sharing, and me taking. The pattern of our friendship was cemented so early on, we never changed course. Until I ended things by moving here. At least I remember that.

"Upset, obviously." She pouts. "You look awful, Wells. Like you've seen a ghost, or worse."

Fire lit, I wince as I stand.

"Wells, you need to sit!" Tippy's cheerful voice requires absolute attention.

"Fine, but can we have tea before you play nurse?"

She walks away without an answer, headed to the bathroom for supplies, I presume. In the kitchen I pull out two mugs, then a third as Freddy joins me. His hair tousled, his sweatshirt on backwards as if he dressed in the dark.

"Wells, it's been too long. Look at your hair! Have they no barbers on this island?" Freddy walks toward me and gives me a half embrace, cognizant of the fact my torso has been injured. "I hear you've got two cracked ribs, are you completely broken up?"

"It's not so bad, really, it's my head that throbs. Damn concussion." I begin pouring the water from the whistling kettle into the mugs. "Tea?"

"Of course," Freddy says, leaning against the wooden countertop and looking me over, pursing his lips. Freddy is tall and broad-shouldered. He played lacrosse in high school, though it's a fact he loathes. He is traditionally handsome with a crooked nose that gives him character and a jawline that makes him appear more serious than he is. "I was royally pissed when you decided not to come home for Christmas," he says, taking the mug of tea from my hand.

"Why didn't I come?" I ask, wondering if it was the business with Tippy lingering — or worsening. Frowning, I add milk to my Earl Grey. "I've always loved Christmas in the city."

We sit at the small table, Tippy joining us with bandages, ointment and a bottle of pills. "You didn't come," she says, kneeling before me and opening the front of my robe, "because you said you were staying with the students and faculty for their *yuletide festivities*."

Her emphasis on the last two words tells me that my choice not to come was more than a little annoying. It was me, then, who declined. Have Tippy and I mended our broken alliance, or is it still in shambles? We had so much air to clear. If my memories return, we could avoid an uncomfortable rehashing. I'd much prefer that. I assume Tippy feels the same, considering she is focused on taking care of me.

"Did you miss me?" I broach as she redresses my bandages.

She looks up at me, her pink lips full, blue eyes wide. I swallow. It's a look I know well. It was that look that had me searching for jobs across the country. I love Tippy, she knows that. But we needed space. Being friends is best.

"Yes, I missed you," she says, opening an orange pill bottle and handing me a dose. "A snowstorm hit the city, and we were forced to stay home. Freddy was a grump. His father was drunk. My mother was needy. I missed you."

Freddy snorts. "Once again, Tippy makes me sound like an ass for no good reason."

"And did you have a reason?" I ask him.

His jaw tenses, eyes on Tippy, then he looks away. "I suppose not. The stress of studying for the bar isn't sufficient reason to mope. Not at Christmas."

"And the *yuletide festivities*?" Tippy asks. "Do you remember anything from the holidays?"

I take a drink of my tea, leaning back in my chair. "None of it."

"How long did the doctors say this amnesia might last?" Freddy asks.

Tippy reaches for the papers the doctor gave us when we left the hospital yesterday afternoon. "It appears his brain scans were fine, no bleeding or cause for alarm there. We are supposed to keep a close eye on him, because of the concussion."

"You aren't answering the question, though." Freddy twists his lips quizzically before asking, "How long until Wells can remember the last six months?"

I run a hand over the base of my neck, exhausted by the last twenty-four hours. Yesterday morning I woke in a Seattle hospital. Evidently, I was flown there after being found on the rocky beach, one part of the sprawling property of Glennmare. Unconscious, bleeding, my clothes torn. A helicopter transferred me to the city, where I was assessed and bandaged up and declared fit enough to leave.

"The doctors hope by the time they see me in two days, some, if not all, of my memories will be recovered," I tell Freddy.

"Have you remembered anything?" he asks.

Ignoring the girl from my dream, in the white gown, hair to her waist, turning from me, I shake my head at my oldest friends. *We must.*

"Nothing," I lie. Because what can I say? It might not even be a memory. I don't *want* it to be a memory.

Because I know where that girl and I were standing when her clothes fell, in my dream. We were in the old cabin. And we weren't alone.

CHAPTER 7. THE GIRLS

We have to tell him, all of us agree.

We need to go to his cottage and explain everything. Then he will be on our side, and we won't be alone with these images dancing in our minds. We will make him share the pain we have to live with.

But what if he does actually remember and is pretending he doesn't to try to protect us?

What do we do then?

We need to stay calm, we take deep breaths. We won't tell anyone anything. You can take secrets to the grave, can't you?

Our collective moan reminds us we're all in this together — all five of us, even if Kitty isn't here. We feel more like sisters than roommates. That is why we did what we did. At least that's what we tell ourselves, because if we start telling the detectives the absolute truth of what happened that night, we might all just break down and never get back up.

Tears fill our eyes.

It was all so wrong, we admit to ourselves.

Does it matter now?

Not really. It's too late for that.

But why isn't she back yet? She should be back by now. Shouldn't she?

We both hate her and love her and our hearts are as mixed up as our minds. If only Friday had never happened. This whole mess would look so different. We are all eighteen, but we've never felt more childlike. How old before this feeling goes away? Does anyone ever feel all grown up?

Kitty did. She always seemed to know exactly who she was.

Which is part of the problem, really; we looked to her for the answers, instead of looking inside ourselves. And now nothing will ever be the same again.

The power is still out, the school freezing, the smell of Johanna's oatmeal not at all tempting us to crawl out of our beds. God, that woman is annoying. Her prying will start the moment we enter the dining hall.

Can we stay here forever and act like nothing happened?

Sure, unless the police get the idea to look in the abandoned cabin.

We destroyed the evidence, we hope.

But we aren't fools. We are teenage girls with fierce eyes and strong wills and the belief in a power other people don't understand. The power of our collective, the power of our hands held tight and secrets whispered in the dead of night. The power of a group of girls who've already been sent out into the world, away from home, to fend for ourselves.

We belong to no one but ourselves.

Well, that isn't entirely true, we think, memories dancing in our eyes. Candlelight and a white mare; an ancient rite and hearts made of glass, so easy to break, a man who couldn't look away.

We do belong to someone, according to the legend.

We won't forget that, even if we are the only ones who remember.

CHAPTER 8. DETECTIVE LEONARD ABBOTT

Detective Phoebe Baker is always on my ass for running late. Today's no different. "What the hell took you so long?" she asks, handing me a to-go paper cup as I slide into her cruiser.

We've worked together for two years, Detective Baker and I, and while sometimes I think I'd prefer to work solo, on mornings like this, where she offers me coffee and a smile that tells me she got plenty of sleep — unlike me — I thank Gordon for giving me a partner with so much energy.

I'm a thirty-eight-year-old single father who's always late because my fifteen-year-old daughter refuses to wake up with the alarm. Getting her to school on time is near impossible.

"Let me guess." Phoebe laughs as she pulls the car out of the police-station parking lot and heads toward the academy. "You gonna use the Cassidy excuse?"

"It's not an excuse. I have to drive her to school when she misses the bus."

"She could walk. You're a pushover."

"It could be worse. I could be a deadbeat who doesn't give a shit about his kid."

"Fair point. Speaking of, you think the parents who send their girls to Glennmare are just happy to be rid of them, or do they think it's actually good for kids to be sequestered from the modern world? I hear they don't even have WiFi out there."

I shrug, taking a sip of the triple americano, with cream. Phoebe picked up my daily order from Whidbey Coffee Company, the only acceptable café on the island. "Toss up, probably. I can't imagine sending Cassidy away to school."

"That's because missing the bus is her worst habit. When I was a teenager, my parents would have sent me there if they'd had the money. I was a beotch."

I chuckle as I look over at Phoebe. She's a twenty-six-year-old black woman with a positive attitude and a friendly smile and is in way better shape than me. We're polar opposites but work well together. "I can't imagine you giving your parents too much grief?"

"I had a lot of growing up to do. How about you, Abbott, were you a boy scout or what?"

"Uh, I went through a rough patch but ironed things out before I graduated high school."

"What's the wildest thing you ever did?" she asks as we turn onto the main road that runs the length of the island.

"Not sure we should go there — might change how you see me."

She flat-out laughs at that. "You think your little island-life antics will shock me?" Laughter grips her and her shoulders shake at the very thought of it. "I grew up in downtown Seattle — pretty sure there was worse trouble there than on this slice of paradise. Try me, or are you too embarrassed, even after all these years?"

"Fine," I say. "I slept with a girl from Glennmare when I was sixteen."

Phoebe whistles. "Damn, Detective, I didn't think you had it in you!"

I shake my head. "Why? Because I'm old?"

"You're not that old. It's your beer belly that makes you seem soft."

"Anyone ever tell you you're an expert at making a compliment seem like a dig?"

"Actually, yes. My mama may have mentioned it a few thousand times." She sips her coffee, then gives me a sidelong glance, her hands on the wheel. "So give me the deets, old man. I want the story of you and this rebel girl from your high-school days."

I tell it to her the same way I told the chief of police. When I finish, she snorts. "Okay, so then you're going to this fancy boarding school today with your mind all made up?"

"I'm just telling you the facts."

"Sure, but you have a bias. I don't want that to interfere with us finding this missing person."

"You saw the tapes from the gas station, right?"

"Yeah." Phoebe nods, turning right onto Glennmare's property. "And?"

"And they make this girl seem shady."

"She's a child," Phoebe says emphatically. "What if it was Cassidy? You'd move heaven and earth for her."

"Fair enough, but I wouldn't have sent her away to some anti-technology, creepy-ass academy in the middle of bum-fuck nowhere."

Phoebe snorts.

"What?" I ask.

"You never get so riled up, is all. You are usually cool and collected. This version of you is pissed."

"How about we call it protective?" I shake my head. "You know most of these girls arrive on the island in a hired car? Their parents don't even fly out to see what sort of place Glennmare is. They put them on a plane and wash their hands of their own flesh and blood."

"Regardless, we've been looking for her for thirty hours, no leads. At all. If there's any chance that she wants to be found, don't we owe it to her to keep looking?"

I exhale, conceding. "When we spoke to the headmaster yesterday, he acted clueless. Think he will have a better story now?"

"He wasn't on the island when she went missing. Maybe he's an old man and you should give him a break. He's like, seventy. And he was in Port Townsend with his grandchildren."

"Missed a hell of a night. You think it's a coincidence?" I ask.

Phoebe Baker turns off her car in the Glennmare Academy parking lot. "Guess it's time to find out. The teacher is back from the hospital."

"I know." I lift my tablet and shake it. "I've been reading all the reports as they come in."

"Wow, I'm impressed. Don't you need readers for that or some shit?"

I shake my head, smiling to myself as we get out of the car. "So if you don't think she ran away, do you think the teacher had something to do with it?"

Phoebe shrugs, tossing her keys in the black leather bag she has slung over her shoulder. "Don't see the connection. Wasn't he out riding a horse, fell, got a concussion and short-term memory loss? What does he have to do with the Katherine Calloway case?"

"I suppose we should ask the girls."

CHAPTER 9. FREDDY

In the guest bedroom, I roll my eyes at Tippy. She stands at the closed door, her right ear pressed against it. The headmaster knocked on the door of Wells' cottage just as we were playing a quiet game of cards in front of the fire. After he asked for a moment alone with his employee, Tippy and I sought refuge in the bedroom where we slept last night.

"Why are you trying to eavesdrop?" I ask her. "He'll just tell us the whole story once the headmaster leaves."

Tippy spins, eyes wide. "Oh, you really think so?"

"Are you referring to the lies he told about where he grew up or the fact that you were secretly sleeping with him on and off for the past few years?"

"Stop," Tippy whisper-yells. "Not now, Freddy. Just. Please."

I flop onto the bed, annoyed with her. Her comment about me being moody over Christmas ticked me off. She knows why I was angry, though of course she isn't going to explain all that to Wells. Especially not now.

"Can you hear anything?" I ask, rolling over on the bed, wedging a pillow beneath my head, closing my eyes. I slept dreadfully last night.

She sighs. "Not if you keep talking." Turning from the door, she lies down beside me. "How long until he remembers, do you think?" she asks.

Eyes closed, I exhale. "Shush. I want to savor each moment we have."

She elbows me. "This is so twisted. He has no idea he hates us."

I smirk. "It's a second chance. Our redemption story."

"The guilt is killing me," she says with a whimper.

"That's what you were doing in Oregon, paying penance?"

"Something like it. I threw out my first draft of the book and started over."

"What's it about now?"

"Love," she says softly.

I open my eyes, turning to look at her. Her eyes are on the still closed door. Anticipating Wells. Like always.

"Look at you, all soft and sentimental," I say, knowing deep down I am the same — syrupy over love, too.

"Hardly." Her head turns; our gazes meet. "I'm growing tired is all."

"How can I help?"

She scoffs. "You can rip my heart right out of my chest and feed it to the horses in the stables."

"Macabre."

"Remember when we took Wells to that bar for his twenty-third birthday? How he got so drunk on Brandy Alexanders and then told us how he'd recently slept with a freshman in the college class he taught?"

"Why are you thinking about that now?" I wonder if it will always be Wells on her mind. Always on my mind, too. Remembering a drunken Wells turns my thoughts to another birthday — his twenty-first. He tried to kiss me that night, not because he liked men, or even liked me — but because he craved a closeness, one I couldn't offer. When I pushed him away, he confessed that there was a hole inside him, one he was desperate to fill. Is it empty still?

25

"Just makes me wonder, is all, about the missing girl," Tippy says, her words as far away as my thoughts. "If he was okay living in the gray then, is he still?"

"What are you really trying to ask?" My tone is now tight, my focus clearer. "I am here to help my oldest friend, not instigate more trouble for him."

"I'm not asking anything. And for the record, he is my oldest friend, too. We met him the same day. And if we are going to get technical, I know him more intimately than you." Tippy rolls off the bed and stands, her hair tousled from lying against the pillows, and I want to reach out and smooth it down, and I hate that I want that. I hate the way my fingers itch to be close to this woman who isn't mine to hold. Who never really was. And I hate that she is putting images in my mind of her and Wells, and the close nature of their friendship.

"Come on, let's interrupt," she says, utterly unaware of how her elfish beauty spins me off my axis, how quickly her words turn me around. She licks her lips. Dammit, maybe she knows exactly what she does to me.

"God, give the man some space. He might be getting put on leave at this very moment. He can't exactly teach while he's out of his mind."

Sometimes Tippy's selfishness grates at me. Mostly it draws me in. Her utter lack of care for any needs but her own. If only I were so bold, what sort of man would I be?

Just then the front door slams and we hear Wells growl. Tippy pulls open the guest room door, moving in search of him. I trail her.

"What happened?" Tippy asks. Wells sits in the center of the couch, facing the fire, hand on his side.

"Can you get me a whiskey, neat?" he asks, looking over at me. "Kitchen pantry, maybe?"

It is only ten in the morning, but I'm not going to question him right now. I find the bottle and a small glass, then bring it to him in the living room. "So what is the verdict?" I ask, pouring the amber liquid. He takes the glass from me and drains it completely.

Wells runs a hand through his black hair, pulling the wavy locks from his dark eyes. Wells is six-foot-three, lean and strong, and seeing him in physical pain is something new. I would say it doesn't suit him, but somehow he carries the look of a wounded hero easily, as if he has been primed for this role all his life.

Wells clears his throat. "He put me on leave until I'm in 'better health.' Which makes sense. I am completely wrecked at the moment." He exhales, looking around the room as if it is as new to him as it is to Tippy and me. Poor man can't remember anything about moving in here, and it shows. Wells clears his throat. "But then he mentioned Katherine, the missing girl."

Tippy frowns. "Why, what do you have to do with the student?"

"The headmaster said she was in my Irish Lit seminar, along with four other girls."

"But why mention her?" I want to know what the headmaster knows. Regretting that I didn't press my ear to the door like Tippy. I might know more now if I had.

Wells twirls the whiskey in his tumbler. "It was odd. He said all the girls, and me, are going to be questioned by the detectives on the case."

Tippy looks over at me.

Wells notices and frowns. "What aren't you saying?" he asks.

I shake my head, ever so slightly, not wanting to get into the fight that ruined so much for us right after he moved to Glennmare. It felt over — our friendship; too many bridges had been burned.

Then the hospital called me. Me. I am his emergency contact, even after all this time. Not Tippy. Me.

"We don't know anything," Tippy says soothingly. "How about I make you a hot toddy? Might be a better use for that whiskey on such a cold morning."

"Sure." Wells sighs, lying down on the couch, a pillow tucked under his head. "God, I'm exhausted." His eyes close and before Tippy finishes boiling the water, he is asleep.

My foot taps the floor, wide awake.

If the police are coming, we need to get the story straight.

CHAPTER 10. JOHANNA

The knock on the back door is unexpected. No one ever fusses with me back here in the kitchen. I pull it open, not sure who to expect.

"No one answered at the front," says a male officer about my age. "I'm Detective Abbott. This is my partner, Detective Baker."

"I'm Johanna Vestige. I do the cooking around here."

"We're looking for the headmaster," Abbott says.

"I think Duncan is out speaking with some faculty." There's no *think* to it. I know he's making the rounds of the cottages, but I pride myself on being discreet, though fair. My loyalty is to Glennmare.

"He is back on the island, then, correct?" Abbott asks.

I nod. "Arrived an hour ago, or so."

"Well, we'd like to speak with you," Detective Abbott says, pulling out a small notepad and pen. "If you don't mind."

My heart swells. They recognize I have valuable insights on the situation, they appreciate that the girls who live here see me as a confidante. That I know things no one else does. I wave the pair toward the warm hearth. "Come in. God knows it's freezing out there."

"You're still without power?" Detective Baker asks, looking around my kitchen. She's a trim woman, short hair, her eyes like a bird, scanning the room for a morsel.

"Yes, though it isn't unusual. My brother tells me I live like a pilgrim out here, but I like it. Quiet, you know?"

"How long have you worked at Glennmare?" Abbott asks.

I sigh. "You're gonna want me to start from the beginning, aren't you?"

The detectives share a look that says yes.

"Fine," I say. "Let's make some coffee then and have cake. I can't handle you pestering me on an empty stomach." Jittering, I add grounds to the French press, and then start the kettle on the gas range, talking quickly as I do. "I have this press because the power goes out so much. Can't work without caffeine. Are you the same?"

Baker smiles. "Actually, yes. We always drive through Whidbey Coffee Company."

I sniff. "That stuff is awful. High prices and watery. And the food is all packaged from the mainland, nothing fresh. Nothing real."

"And what you make here, is it all from scratch?" Abbott asks, taking a seat at the small table in the corner where I usually eat my meals, alone. Though I've asked some of the girls to join me, they never do.

I nod proudly, wiping my hands on my apron. "Of course. I want to make sure the girls are healthy, growing." I slice up the spiced bundt cake I made a few days ago and place the pieces on plates, then walk to the table, offering them to the detectives.

"Wasn't expecting this hospitality," Abbott says, tucking in.

I plunge the press, considering his words. "Why is that?"

He runs a napkin over his mouth, shrugs. "Glennmare seems to keep to itself. Staff included."

"There's a school to run. The girls keep us busy."

"And I imagine you stay pretty busy with keeping food on the table for all the students. Enrollment is at about fifty this year, isn't it?" Abbott asks, though I am sure he already knows. If he doesn't, he's a piss-poor detective.

"Yes, forty-six at the moment, split between four grades. There are five teachers on staff. They each take a subject or two."

"And how long have you worked at Glennmare?" Baker asks me.

I take a bite of the cake. "About two years. Moved here from Boise." After losing my girl, I was desperate to begin again. Now, I see Matilda's ghost everywhere, which is how I like it. I don't want to forget. Having the girls around, needing me, is what keeps me from going to the dark place where I lived after Matilda's death.

Abbott smiles. "Another native Pacific Northwesterner, don't get too many of them here at Glennmare."

My eyes narrow. "What do you know of Glennmare?"

Abbott adjusts in his seat, clears his throat. "I know that a girl is missing, and we need to find her."

"Speaking of the girls, tell us about them," Baker says.

"All of them?" I ask, eyebrows raised.

Baker smirks. "Specifically, Katherine Calloway."

"Kitty is special." I pour the rich coffee into three mugs, averting my eyes.

"I don't doubt it," Abbott says. "I read in the report that she's an accomplished horse rider."

"All the girls here are. That isn't what sets her apart."

"Then what is it?" Baker asks, pen in hand, ready to write down whatever I say. I smile, thinking I could tell them anything. And what would they know? I may not be from this island, but I've lived at Glennmare for two years and know its secrets. Know what to keep safe. "Have you spoken with her parents?"

The detectives both nod. "Yes," Baker says. "They've been at the station and gone out with the search party. They are rightfully concerned."

I scoff. "Well, you'll never find Kitty by talking to her folks. They have their heads up their rears, pardon my French."

"Why do you say that?"

I lean back in my chair, taking a sip of the coffee. It's good. "Some girls who come here have parents who are concerned. Want the best for their daughters, a solid education."

"And other parents?" Abbott asks, elbows on the table, curious.

"Most of these parents pay for out of sight, out of mind. I can't respect those sorts. How could you forget about your own child?"

"Maybe some parents hoped that being on an island, without access to technology, would keep a child on the straight and narrow? Maybe Katherine's parents had a reason to send her here. They mentioned she had run away quite a bit, before moving to Glennmare. Is this something that concerns you?"

I shake my head. "I wouldn't be concerned with that."

"You seem rather calm, considering a student you call special has gone missing. Are you not worried?" Baker asks, her eyes quizzical.

But she is only confused because she doesn't know. Doesn't understand. Kitty and her friends are different from other girls at Glennmare. Different than girls anywhere. They don't run.

They hide.

CHAPTER 11. THE GIRLS

The detectives are on the property. We saw them pull up the long drive. It's why we snuck down the back stairwell and went straight for the stables. We saddled up Petunia, Gardenia, Tansy and Iris — we all have a horse of our own. Violet belonged to Kitty, and we feed her an apple, petting her brown nose. She must miss Kitty as much as we do. We miss Lily too, Wells' favorite white mare, though he would take out the black stallion if he was doing anything more than a trot.

Lily belongs here with the other mares but will never be here again.

Standing here, in the stables, has us clutching one another's hands. Looking into each other's eyes, haunted, horrified, hating who we are.

But the horses shouldn't suffer because we are callous and cold. Still, it feels wrong, knowing what we know, to take them from the stables, to offer them anything at all. If they knew, they would hate us too.

We lift into stirrups, our white dresses flowing down to our ankles, thick woolen coats buttoned high. Hands mittened. We open the stable door and escape.

Past Glennmare, through the back fields, toward the water.

It still doesn't seem real. That Kitty is gone and Professor Wells has forgotten and the night is over. All that heartache for nothing. We stare into the water, wanting to remember the good times — but all our memories feel centered on Kitty, and we let her down. She wanted more than we could give and now it feels as if we have failed her.

We thought saying yes enough times would cement our love, but now we doubt that is how love works at all.

We should go back to the academy. We've been riding an hour — more. We know that, but we can't stop. We ride on, the horses' hooves on the solitary, sandy shore of the island. Galloping over the icy break of water, our hair whips in the wind.

Should we go to him?

We want to.

Badly.

We move toward the trail, without thinking, without debate. It's all too fresh to push aside.

A mile from the academy, in the woods, is the dilapidated cabin that has been our little hidden sanctuary. We circle the abandoned well that is flush with the ground, covered with a plank of wood, with rocks, with leaves. The horses neigh, wanting to leave.

We understand why.

No one can discover what we've buried.

Salty tears on our cheeks, the same as the ocean, and it doesn't seem fair. None of it.

But nothing was ever fair for us, except for those months last fall, when everything felt like it made sense for the first time in forever. But there is nothing here now.

We turn back to Glennmare, wishing the Kitty we knew was riding with us, knowing when the detectives ask where she is, we won't be able to answer.

CHAPTER 12. DETECTIVE LEONARD ABBOTT

Johanna's full of shit, I know it before she even begins to speak.

Everything she says belies how important she thinks she is. She thinks the girls are her confidantes, but every student we spoke with yesterday said Johanna is a busybody who always tries to be their best friend.

Johanna thinks she holds a winning hand of cards, but she's playing a game where she's the fool. We won't get anywhere by drinking coffee in this kitchen.

"We need to speak with the headmaster," I say, standing. "Do you think you can direct us to him?"

"You can always wait in the hall, outside his office."

"Fine," I say. "Thank you for your time, much appreciated."

"Anything I can do to help Kitty," she says, docile. Pandering. Fake as hell.

We enter the lobby, where large staircases on both the left and the right lead to the second story, which has a balcony. Students look over the edge, whispering. They are dressed in blazers and khakis, pleated skirts. They look like they could be students at any private school in the country.

A woman greets us, smiling. "You're the detectives?" she asks. "Looking for Katherine?" Her auburn hair is pulled back into a low bun. She is tall and lean with soft features and wears small gold earrings. She's about Phoebe's age, wearing dark jeans, a white T-shirt and a plaid suit coat.

"Yes," I say, introducing us. "And you are?"

"Melinda Ellis, the math teacher. I am so glad you are both on this case." She shakes her head. "Poor thing, she was so dear. So kind."

"Could you tell us more about her?" Phoebe asks. "Anything might help."

Melinda nods. "Of course, my office is on the second floor."

As we move through the lobby, I note the elaborate arrangement of flowers on a front table, the umbrella stand full, the large mirror polished to a shine, gilded. No dust, no cobwebs. I was picturing a dilapidated school, but this building could be used as a set for a period piece.

"For a technology-free school, everything looks so pristine," I say. "Everything is so clean."

Melinda turns and smiles. "That's the charm, I suppose. Without screens, the girls have plenty of time to do their chores."

"What sorts of chores?" Phoebe asks.

We follow Melinda up the wide wooden staircase. I take in the academy as we walk. The walls are lined with portraits of people long dead. "The girls have a list of daily chores — tasks to keep them strong and resilient — that is what keeps the school and property in such tiptop shape."

On the landing, we see a framed piece of embroidery. "*Idle hands are the devil's tools*," Phoebe reads aloud. "Intense."

"The founders of the school were traditional," Melinda explains. "And they weren't just anti-technology, they also believed young women should work hard and be diligent in all endeavors."

"Is that still the school's creed?" I ask as Melinda opens an oak door in an empty hall.

She twists her lips as we enter her office. "Honestly, I wouldn't say so. The students now have plenty of freedom.

35

I am still getting used to how much time they have to themselves." She shakes her head at this thought, then directs us to sit.

Her office is big enough for a desk and chair, plus a sitting area with a couch and two armchairs, a coffee table with a teapot, and two empty teacups. She has books piled everywhere, candles, and I notice a decanter filled with a rich amber liquid on a sideboard. We sit on the couch and watch as Melinda goes to her desk, rummaging through files.

"So, one positive of not having computers on campus is I have gotten really good with taking notes."

"The teachers don't even get them?" I ask, surprised.

"Nope. It is a drawback for a lot of people, for sure. I have my cellphone, but reception is rough. I have to go to the public library to get WiFi."

"You must be pretty dedicated to this school to deal with that," Phoebe says.

Melinda sits down in an armchair, shaking her head. "Dedicated is one word. But I think most people here are escaping something."

"What are you running from?" I ask her, resting my forearms on my knees, leaning in, curious.

"I was tired of trying to keep up. Miserable in San Francisco. Everything was so expensive. Rent especially. I had three roommates, I could hardly afford a latte on the weekends, and I was buried in student loan debt. Public-school teachers make a decent living if they aren't living in a big city. But I felt swamped."

"How did you find Glennmare?" I ask.

"A lot of parents in the Bay area are worried about how much time their kids spend online, how addicting it can be. I was looking into different approaches to teaching to better serve those families. As I was researching, I read about Glennmare in an article on radical approaches to education and decided it was time to make a change. I started here this fall, same as Wells Halifax."

"And are you happy here?" I ask.

She nods, giving us a crooked smile. "I have been. The island is gorgeous, the pay is absurd, and the students are very engaged in their learning."

"Was Katherine Calloway equally as interested as her peers?"

Melinda smiles. "More than most students. Her friend group is . . . dedicated. They felt the creed of the school should apply to more than just eliminating technology. They wanted to go back in time."

"How so?" Phoebe asks.

Melinda leans back in her chair. "You've seen them, right? Katherine's girlfriends?"

I shake my head. "We haven't. They were interviewed by the chief of police yesterday."

"Well, you won't miss them. Long white dresses, stockings, wool coats and ribbons in their hair. They go home for break and meticulously put together wardrobes that fit the aesthetic here. And they have money to do it."

Phoebe smirks. "Seriously?"

Melinda nods. "Absolutely. The skirts and lace collars and pearls are all intentional. I thought it was some sort of dress code when I got here, but it's just those five girls that wear those costumes. It's all a choice, the clothes they wear, how they talk, move. They love it here. And maybe it's in part because of the freedom from their parents, but it's like they've been given this chance to turn back time. Imagine your teenage years. You didn't have a mini-computer in your pocket. Back then you were probably more creative, more—"

"Delinquent," I say with a snort. "I don't know, I have a teenage daughter and cannot imagine her playing dress-up like the girls you mention."

Melinda nods. "I get that. And sure, there's trouble that happens on occasion, but Kitty is a sweet girl who just wants to play make-believe, her friends too. No one cares how they choose to dress. That's the beauty of Glennmare. The girls here don't have to pretend. They can just *be*."

Phoebe shakes her head, not buying it. "And when they can *just be* they turn into the *Dead Poets Society* á la *Little Women*?"

Melinda opens the folder in her lap. "I'm not making up how much Kitty and her friends love it here. Read this. It's Kitty's response to how she felt after summer break. I'm her homeroom teacher too."

She hands me the piece of lined paper. I read the cursive, Phoebe reading over my shoulder.

> *Being back at Glennmare is like coming home. Summer break was exhausting. My parents fought. My brothers bickered. And I was all alone. Dreaming of my best friends, of Diane and Coretta, Bernie and Jolie. I just wanted to be back in our dorm room where we agonized over ridiculous decisions like what we might wear to class on the first day and what new teacher Headmaster Duncan might have hired. Even though we get a little jealous at times and have all been vying for the same person's attention, I love them like sisters. The worst part of coming back was knowing it is my last year of high school. I never want this to end. Never, ever.*

"Doesn't sound like a girl who would run away, does it?" Melinda asks when we finish reading.

"No, it doesn't," I say. "What else do you know of Kitty?"

"She was the leader of her friend group, everyone adored her. It's crazy, though. I spoke with her parents yesterday, at their hotel in town, and they didn't seem to know the Kitty I knew."

I nod in agreement to her assessment. "We spoke with them too."

She exhales. "I would describe them as cold, to be honest. I heard they didn't want to come here, didn't want to see her room, look through her things. They completely shut off their emotions."

Melinda's description damn near exactly matches our experiences when speaking with the Calloways. They considered

Kitty to be an eighteen-year-old woman who always played her own games. This was just another in a long string.

"So how did they describe their daughter to you?" Phoebe asks.

"They thought it was just like her to be brash and irreverent, to make a mess of things," Melinda says. "But the Kitty I knew . . . she was generous, she would bring me tea in the afternoons, she would ask me to check her math work and could always be found braiding some classmate's hair or cutting flowers in the garden. The girls would get possessive of one another at times, but never about anyone else."

"Possessive how?" Phoebe asks.

"Possessive with one another. They never spent time with other students. They only ever had eyes for themselves."

Curious, I ask, "Were any of them dating each other?"

Melinda shrugs. "I don't know. I think they were all a little bit in love, but with who, I don't know."

"Everyone comes to this school for a reason. Do you know what Katherine's reason was?" I ask.

Melinda runs a hand over the back of her neck. "She mentioned it, briefly. It sounds like she'd fallen in love with an older man, and her parents were angry. She came here because she was sent away."

"And while here, did she repeat this pattern, you think?" Phoebe asks.

Melinda shrugs. "I can't say. I've been so wrapped up in learning my way around this academy, and I helped plan the yuletide festivities and I had to make lesson plans. I don't know. I really just know what I've seen. And what I've seen amounts to Katherine Calloway being a charmer." Melinda shrugs. "She charmed me."

* * *

After leaving Melinda's office, we head to the foyer to find Duncan, the headmaster. I know who he is because he's lived on the island for a decade, but we've never had a reason to talk. Now, things are different.

"My office," he says, opening the door for us. Phoebe and I follow him in, sitting opposite his desk.

He jumps right in. "I take it you met Johanna?"

"Yes, she was courteous, but reserved," Phoebe tells Duncan. "We did a background check on her before we came in this morning. Does she ever mention her deceased daughter? She died when she was in high school."

I appreciate my partner's ability to cut to the chase. Why she's on this island instead of working cases in a big city is beyond me. She says she wanted a slower pace of life. I don't push her on why, but I get the feeling she was burned pretty badly by the last man she dated. We all have things we wish to escape; she just did a better job of escaping them than me. I see my ex-wife every time I walk into the supermarket.

"Johanna never talks about her girl. Tragic, really. Suicide." He sighs, running a hand over his jaw. "She is a bit needy, though. I always seem to be on eggshells around her." His hair is silver, skin pink, and he has a white beard reminiscent of Old Saint Nick. "She's loyal. I'll give her that."

We introduce ourselves, and I look around his office as he waxes poetic about *serving families in crisis* and *doing the work that needs to be done*. He isn't a minister, so I am not sure where this holier-than-thou attitude is coming from. How does this old man actually relate to his students? Not that I have the best pulse on relevancy, but still. I have Phoebe to thank for keeping me up to speed on what apps are cool and what television shows to watch so Cassidy doesn't think I'm too much of a loser. And I must be half this man's age.

Duncan's office has a wall of filled bookshelves. Not a device in sight. I wonder how he keeps track of his students without a computer database. The anti-technology rhetoric appears to be real.

"We've been told you were off the island two nights ago, when Katherine went missing. Can you tell us more about what you were doing?" I ask.

Duncan clears his throat, leaning back in his chair. "I was with my family in Port Townsend. My grandson was competing in a basketball game. Sadly, they lost."

"Is this something you do regularly? Leave?"

"On occasion. While I am Headmaster, I am also from the Peninsula, and I wouldn't want to miss family events. Especially now that my wife has passed. Are you a family man, Detective?" He addresses me, completely omitting Phoebe from the conversation.

"Yes, my daughter Cassidy is a sophomore at Oak Harbor High School."

"Ah, wonderful. Is she happy at that institution? You may not know this, but we have room here, at Glennmare, if she is interested."

I chuckle. "The monthly tuition here is more than my detective's salary can afford."

"We have scholarships. Some especially for islanders, though we've never had a family take us up on it."

"Is that so?" My tone is flat. I would never send my daughter here — not because I find fault with the school. Actually, after speaking with Melinda, my instincts tell me this place is good for many kids. Just not my kid. I wouldn't send my daughter to this campus when our comfortable one-story, three-bedroom house is fifteen minutes away.

"We're here to gain more information on Katherine Calloway," Phoebe says. "I know you've cooperated with the officers that were called in on the case yesterday, but since we are looking at thirty-plus hours since she has gone missing, it's growing more serious by the minute."

Duncan leans forward, nodding. "I agree. And I am willing to cooperate fully. From my end, I suggest you interview Wells Halifax."

"The teacher?" I ask. "That is the same man who was in the horse accident and was sent to Harborview by helicopter?"

Duncan nods. "Wells Halifax. He taught a seminar on Irish Lit to a group of upperclassmen last semester. Johanna has informed me that the students and Mr. Halifax spent time outside the classroom together."

"What are you suggesting?"

Duncan raises his hands. "Nothing at all. But he may know something about Katherine, or the girls he taught may, that no one else has considered. There were only five of them in the class. And they all share a dormitory."

"What did Johanna say they did outside of the classroom, this group?" Phoebe asks.

"Ride horses together, mostly. Wells is also in charge of the stables. It's one of the reasons we hired him. We tend to hire staff who can work in more than one discipline."

"And where do you think Katherine is?" I ask. "Was there a reason she may have wanted to leave Glennmare?"

"I would guess she took a ferry somewhere, thinking no one would notice. She left on a Friday night. I would think she was rebelling, as is the tendency with many girls. Of course, she is a legal adult. Maybe she was ready to move on?"

Phoebe tenses beside me. "Sir, is there a problem the police aren't aware of? Have other girls from Glennmare left like this?"

"Don't read into it. Teenagers like to throw caution to the wind. I raised four children, I should know."

"You seem rather calm, considering the situation," I say, frustrated at this man's lack of concern.

Duncan shakes his head. "To the contrary. I am worried, but within reason."

With a clenched jaw, I stand. "And out of curiosity, when will you begin to display more concern?"

"She will be back before classes start tomorrow, I'm sure of it. It's Sunday morning. She may very well be on a ferry home right now."

Phoebe presses her lips in a firm line. "For your sake, I hope she is."

CHAPTER 13. WELLS

After the headmaster visited to place me on leave, I fell into a deep sleep. The visions in my dreams had me rattled. Again, the girl in white. But now she was naked. I couldn't see her face, but the curve of her bare back was seared into my memories. In my dreams I begged her to turn, to lift her chin. She refused.

The knocking on the front door startles me from my reveries.

I stumble to the living room, where a pair of uniformed police officers are eyeing Freddy. Tippy offers them tea as I attempt to orientate myself to the situation.

"Thank you, but we already had coffee," Abbott declines. "With Johanna."

"That's the woman who found me, right?" I ask. I sprawl out on the couch, my ribs too sore to sit upright. The detectives sit in armchairs on either side of the blazing fire.

"Found you?" Detective Abbott asks.

"Yes, and thank God she was out on a walk," Tippy says, looking over at me sympathetically. "Otherwise, you'd have been washed out to sea."

"For the last twenty-four hours we were working to find Katherine but didn't have reason to believe the situations were linked."

"Has that changed?" I ask, indignant. What character assassination is this?

"Johanna had some interesting opinions about you," Detective Baker says. "Considering she saved your life."

"Are you trying to bait me? Because I don't remember what happened, or who this Katherine girl is. Though I'm certainly sorry to hear she is missing."

Just then the lights flicker on, and the sound of the heater kicking back up causes us all to brighten. "Finally." Freddy exhales. "One night here and I'm ready to leave. If it wasn't for you, old friend, I would already be gone. This place is downright ancient."

Detective Abbott lifts a brow at that. "I take it you've never visited?"

I look to Tippy and Freddy, not knowing the answer but guessing it. I *do* remember the shouting match I shared with Tippy, on the tennis courts of the club, last July. The sky blue, preparing for the fireworks that would come when the day turned to night. The holiday promised freedom, offering us a reprieve from all the things we both held so tight to our chests. Our pent-up words began volleying with such speed that we were asked to leave. It was then I decided to look for a position as far away as possible. I landed here. I remember all that — just not the after.

"Never made it out, I'm afraid. It was a busy fall." Freddy smiles politely. "I'm in law school." He pauses. "We had hoped for some time this spring, but, now, well, here we are."

I run a hand over my bandaged side. Tired. "What is it you would like to know, specifically?" I ask the detectives. "I want to help, though I'm not sure how, considering I can't remember a single thing that has transpired since I moved here."

"Well, it's an interesting coincidence, your accident occurring the same night Katherine went missing," Detective Baker states.

"What are you insinuating?" Tippy asks, pouring Freddy a cup of tea from the pot on the coffee table.

"In all the time I've worked on this island, I've never had a case at Glennmare. And now, two incidents on the same evening. You don't find that odd?"

"Of course it's odd," I say. I'm beginning to get short with them.

"There is talk of foul play," Detective Baker says. Finally, someone willing to cut to the chase.

"What sort of foul play?" Freddy asks, leaning in.

"There is no record of her leaving the island, according to the ferry terminal footage."

"She could have bypassed the ferries, gone north, over Deception Pass," Tippy says.

"Possibly," Detective Baker says.

"If you are thinking foul play, do you have suspects?" I ask. "Is that why you're here?"

Detective Baker eyes me with more consideration. "Why do you think we are here?"

"The student — Katherine — was in one of my classes. Duncan told me. But I don't remember anything of this school year." I point to the papers on the coffee table. "Have a look at those. The doctors are confident my memory will return in the next few days. Perhaps I can be of more assistance then."

Detective Abbott takes the paperwork, begins to read.

"A missing girl is a serious matter," Detective Baker says, lips pursed. She lifts her naturally arched brow. "Have you remembered something?"

I shake my head, focusing on the matter at hand, agitated at their need for a narrative I cannot supply. "Of course a missing person is urgent business. I just don't know how I can be of help."

Detective Baker reaches for her side. But she isn't pulling out a gun. No, she pulls out her phone, taps the screen. She reveals it to me. "Do you remember her?" she asks. "This is Katherine Calloway."

My jaw tenses, my eyes remain steady.

The girl in my dreams, who wouldn't turn, who refused to show me her face, is now staring back at me.

CHAPTER 14. FREDDY

Alone, outside Wells' pitiful cottage, I take a deep breath of the icy island air. Tippy is inside doting over Wells, as should be expected, but it is difficult to watch. She knows how it hurts me.

That makes me sound weak, but I don't know if I care anymore. I wanted what I couldn't have and she made that clear. Only, it took sleeping together for her to come to the conclusion that I wasn't, after all, the man she wanted.

It isn't some clichéd love triangle, it's more nuanced than that. I would say I regret it, but I don't. I would have moved mountains to be with her, as impractical as the step-sibling component made things. And *that* is the reason I was moody at Christmas — Tippy told me we were through. She was moving on.

Now, we are all bunking together in a two-bedroom cottage. Last night I assumed Tippy would share the bed with me, as we've done countless times — but she opted for the couch, claiming she was going to tend to the fire, but God knows she's never stoked a flame in her damn life. She's from Madison Park, and she's never even been camping.

Lighting a cigarette, I look toward the water. In the distance there is a group of horses, their riders dressed in white, long hair whipping in the wind. I inhale, looking for the stables. Walking toward the big barn painted in white, I think about Wells' accident. He fell off a horse and became concussed. He was found by Johanna the cook, who was taking a night stroll.

If she were involved in any of this, why would she have called the police? It would be unlikely. And the detectives didn't even appear to know Johanna was the one who found Wells. Though to be fair they weren't linking the situations until now.

Veering away from the barn, I turn right toward the academy, noticing a woman through the windows in the back. Through the glass window I see a blazing fire, several bare chickens ready to be roasted. The woman is chopping onions and carrots and throwing them into a huge pot.

I pause, watching her work, wondering what it would be like to have such a simple life. Making a homecooked meal in solitude. Have I made all the wrong choices, leading me to a life I barely even want? What would it be like to remove all pressure, all expectations, and make a life where the most pressing issue was how much salt and pepper to use on the vegetables?

I rap my knuckles on the old wooden door, feeling an urge to speak with her.

She looks up when she hears my knock and wipes her hands across her filthy apron before opening the door. "Another detective poking around?"

I shake my head. "No, just a visitor. I'm Frederick."

"Johanna," she says cautiously. "Are you a reporter?"

"No, I'm a friend of Wells Halifax. I just came to town to help nurse him back to health and I heard we owe you a thank you."

"Thank me?" The woman scoffs. "I just did my duty, same as anyone would."

"Do you always take walks at night?" I ask, waiting to be asked in from the cold.

She nods. "Yes, especially if the girls are out on a night ride. I worry about them."

"Which girls go riding at night?"

Johanna's frown softens. "Always the same girls. Katherine and her friends."

"The girls in Wells' seminar?"

She presses her lips together. "I don't particularly like that connection, no offense."

"You don't like Wells?" I ask pointedly.

"He is a little self-assured. Confidence bordering on cockiness. The girls adore him, which makes me nervous. Too handsome for his own good. I know how men can be with pretty women. *Underage women.*"

My eyes widen, taken aback by these words. "Quite the statement."

Johanna shrugs. "I suppose they are all of age now. They are seniors; Kitty was the last of the group to turn eighteen, in December."

"Did you tell the police this, what you're insinuating?"

Johanna shrugs. "I may not like that friend of yours, but my loyalty is to Glennmare. It isn't my business if he works here, but I don't want the academy's name tarnished. So, no, I didn't mention it. Would you like me to?"

I lift my hands in defense. "What are you insinuating? Even if the girls are all eighteen, it is wildly inappropriate for anything to have happened between a student and teacher. And your comments have no basis. I don't see what you're trying to suggest besides stirring the pot. And for the sake of his reputation, I do wish he could clear the air for us to put a stop to unfounded rumors."

"Convenient time to lose one's memories, eh?"

I balk at this. "Are you kidding? Wells' recovery is being overseen by a reputable doctor. If you think he is faking the amnesia, then you ought to take that up with his physician."

Johanna crosses her arms. "If Wells can't remember, the girls still can. Have you asked them about what happened that night?"

I frown, considering her words. "I haven't spoken with them, but why would I? There's no reason to link the events that happened that night. Is there?"

Johanna's cheeks go pink. "I don't know. Haven't had a chance to speak with them yet. The girls are still so shaken. They're terribly worried for their friend."

"As am I." I tip my hat to her, then turn on my heel. That woman is downright delusional. Judging and making accusations and forming opinions based on zero fact.

Makes me wonder what my own opinions are based upon. Reality or fiction? Wells entered my life under false pretenses. But in truth, I was hiding something for a long time too — my devotion to Tippy. But harboring a crush is not in the same orbit as having something to do with a missing girl.

Still, the words of the detectives and Johanna regarding Wells' relationship with his students sends a chill down my spine.

I turn toward the stables, seeing the group of girls dismounting from their horses. Their clothing instantly sets them apart. Lace-hemmed dresses and tall leather boots and scarves wrapped around their necks, long wool capes skimming the dirty floor of the barn. Tippy would love the way these girls dress — always with a flair for fashion herself.

But these girls don't just look like they belong at Oxford eighty years ago — which is what Tippy is usually trying to achieve with her clothing choices, in button-down shirts and trousers. These girls are distinctly romantic, with long ribbons in their hair and billowing blouses.

"Hello," I say, offering a wave. It's mid-afternoon, fog settling low in the gray sky. "May I speak with you?"

"Depends," one of them says. She is tall, demanding attention, with translucent skin, and straight hair, so pale it's almost white, down to her waist.

The four girls look at me with blazing eyes, as if looking for a fight.

"On what?"

"Are you a cop?" the shortest girl asks. Her curly hair is a rich copper, her eyes emeralds. She has on a waistcoat. Where does one even find such a thing?

"Not even a little." I run a hand over my jaw, assessing these girls. They are women, really.

"Who are you then?" a girl with jet-black hair asks. Her tone is brazen; she's clearly very protective of the situation.

"Freddy. A friend of your teacher, Mr. Halifax."

"I've heard of you." A girl narrows her hazel eyes at me. Her Colombian accent is thick. "You went to college with Wells."

"On a first-name basis with your teacher?"

The girls share a look. A look that says they've shared much more than his name. Fuck. What has Wells done this time?

CHAPTER 15. THE GIRLS

Freddy is nothing like Wells. He is calculating and looked at us with judgment. As if we were the ones who caused the accident. We didn't cause anything. We weren't the one who was obsessed. We didn't bring the gun.

Back in our dormitory, we collectively feel the weight of the weekend. Everything is caving in.

"She should be back by now," Jolie whispers as she leans down to tie the laces of her leather boots. Jolie is an heiress but would rather people know she has two priors.

Bernie leans into a mirror propped over her dresser, applying her lip gloss. "We should have gone with her. What sort of friends are we?" Our choice to stay at Glennmare when Kitty left gnaws at us.

Coretta pulls out a bin from under her bed with Korean treats her grandmother sends her each month. Unwrapping a Choco Pie, she sighs. "Maybe she needed to stay at a hotel?"

"Why wouldn't she have called, though?" Diane asks. She may look like a Viking princess, but she is too frail to lead. This morning she was sad. Now she is scared. "That isn't like her. We need to talk to Wells. Maybe he is pretending to have amnesia to protect us. Protect her."

"Well, that would be the most romantic thing ever," Coretta says, eyes sparkling.

"You can still see romance after everything?" Bernie's words are filled with regret. "We need to focus, get our heads out of the clouds."

"That's the most depressing sentence you've ever said," Jolie says, pulling out her box of contraband. She takes out a sheet of rolling paper and sprinkles in a line of pot.

"Johanna will give you an hour on the grounds if she catches you with that," Bernie says.

"Since when do you care about Johanna's detentions?" Jolie snorts. "That hag can go to hell for all I care. She's a total creeper."

"Don't get mean." Coretta moans as she falls into bed. "Eat something sweet. It will make you feel better, I promise." She shoves the bin of treats at Jolie. But Jolie just opens the bedroom window and lights her joint.

"I say we go find Wells," Diane says, standing, fluffing her petticoat. "Before the detectives corner us. I can't go through what we did yesterday with the police."

"We told them everything we knew when we were at the station," Bernie says.

Jolie smirks. "You think they bought it?"

"Why wouldn't they? We're just girls, after all," Coretta says, rolling over in her bed, her head hanging off it, her black hair sweeping the floor.

"If something happens to Kitty . . . and we could have helped her . . . I don't want to live with that," Diane says. Her resolve is fading the fastest.

"What could have happened?" Jolie asks, her voice filled with defeat.

"I don't know . . . she should be here by now," Diane says tearfully. "There is no good reason why she isn't. And I keep worrying that someone is going to start asking what happened to—"

"Don't!" Coretta cries. "Don't say any more. It's all too much."

"But it happened. One minute living and breathing, the next, dead." Diane's words are pragmatic, but the tears in her eyes reveal a more sensitive take on the situation.

"I don't want to think about it," Jolie mutters.

"You want to think about Wells instead? Is he still mad at us? Like, if he could remember that night, would he be?" Bernie asks, buttoning up a white collared shirt, placing a black cap on her head and putting on an oversized duster that falls to her feet.

"He was livid." Diane sits next to Jolie, taking the joint from her friend's fingers. She pulls in a long puff, holds it, then exhales slowly.

"He will be so mad when he remembers," Coretta says with a whimper.

"Don't do that," Jolie says, turning her head of red curls and revealing tears in her green eyes. "I don't want to think about any of this. It's too awful. I just keep thinking how Kitty wasn't herself when she left . . . what if she did something she can't take back?"

"But Kitty wasn't herself for so long . . . you know how she would swing. So happy one minute, angry the next. It was hard to keep up," Coretta says.

Bernie flares. "What are you getting at? Now you are questioning Kitty?"

Jolie smirks. "Maybe you still have a thing for her. Protective much?"

"Kitty and I never had a thing," Bernie says. But the tension in the room reveals Bernie's desire.

"That is what Eli said too, but we know that wasn't true," Diane says, her words uncharacteristically pointed. Cruel.

Coretta squints. "Don't talk about him."

"Why?" Diana spins her hair in her fingers, twisting it into a bun on the top of her head.

"Because he is gone, just like Kitty."

"Wells is as good as gone, too," Bernie says, shaking her head.

"We should go talk to him." Diane stands, wrapping a hand-knitted scarf around her long, pale neck. "We go get answers. There is no one else who might know anything."

"And if he truly doesn't remember?" Bernie asks.

Jolie's eyes turn cold. "We keep lying until he does."

We nod, knowing it's our only choice. Knowing that eventually, he will remember *everything*.

We just hope Kitty is back by then.

CHAPTER 16. DETECTIVE LEONARD ABBOTT

After leaving Wells Halifax's cottage, we walk the property, trying to understand the academy better, thinking we must be overlooking something considering we've gotten nowhere. We pass the stables, the gardens. There is an outbuilding with a pottery studio, a dance studio and a small theater. Touring the grounds, I feel privilege everywhere. The property is landscaped beautifully, and we meet two full-time groundskeepers who are repairing a broken gate. This place is so full of money. What sort of trouble might Katherine Calloway have gotten into here, so far from the rest of the world?

We're standing at the shore, on the edge of Glennmare, overlooking Penn Cove, when my walkie-talkie barks. It's Mikey. "Abbott, give me a call. Got something."

Phoebe turns to me. "Well, call him."

He picks up right away. "What is it?" I ask. Mikey is a patrolman here on the island and a cop I trust.

"We got a guy here who admits to selling Katherine Calloway alcohol. Says he saw her on Friday. I've got him waiting in the back room of the convenience store ready for questioning. What do you want me to do — take him in or you come here?"

"Take him in. We'll be there soon. We're over at Glennmare right now."

I shove my phone in my back pocket. "Guess we should head out."

Phoebe nods and we turn, but a group of four young women cause us to pause. They aren't the first insular-looking group of girls we've seen today, out here — there are dozens of teenagers about the property — but this group is different. They have a singularity about them. Their clothing is completely different for one. But they are also walking with intention. Toward the cottages.

"Those are the girls, Katherine's friends," Phoebe says.

We walk toward them. The officers on duty yesterday questioned them already, but that was before we were assigned to the case. We tried to speak with them earlier, but they were nowhere to be found. Now, here they are.

"Excuse us," Phoebe says once we reach them, pulling out her badge. "We need to speak with you."

"You don't even know who we are," one of them says.

"Of course we do," Phoebe says with a tight smile. "I'm Detective Baker with the Oak Harbor Police Department. This is Detective Abbott."

The girls lift their eyebrows collectively. Not trusting us, at all. With reason. Why would these girls trust anyone after their own parents sent them away?

"I'm Coretta," one says. "This is Jolie, Bernie and Diane. And we spoke with the police yesterday. And with Kitty's parents. And the headmaster. We have nothing more to say to you."

"Where are you headed now?" Phoebe asks. "The home of Wells Halifax?"

The girls stiffen. "It's none of your business," Bernie says. "And if you want to keep talking to us, we will need our lawyers present."

The other girls laugh, but their eyes tell me they are scared. Jolie is smoking a cigarette with feigned nonchalance; Bernie nervously shuffles a deck of tarot cards as we stand staring one another down. All of it comes across as false bravado.

"What do you want from us?" Jolie asks as she stomps out the cigarette with the toe of her boot. Her eyes are bloodshot, which tells me she has her defenses down, perhaps more than her friends.

"We want to know where Katherine Calloway is. Your roommate and classmate," I say plainly. "Can you give us any insight into her whereabouts? Because after forty-eight hours, rarely does a missing person turn back up, and we're inching toward that timeline. If you want that on your conscience, that's on you."

Diane, the tallest girl, wipes a tear from her eye. She pushes her white-blonde hair behind her ear. "Is that true? That statistic?"

Phoebe clears her throat. "Sadly, yes. And this is not to scare you, it is to encourage you to speak up for your friend's safety. There are police all over this island searching for her. Her parents are worried sick. If you know anything—"

"Fine." Diane's voice trembles , shaking her head, tears on her cheeks. "She went to have an abortion, okay?"

"Damn," Jolie says, her words soft. She immediately reaches for Diane and wraps her in an embrace.

"I'm sorry, I wasn't going to say anything, but . . ." Diane sobs as the girls all wrap their arms around her. As if refusing to be anywhere but on the exact same page.

I look over at Phoebe, who has her notepad out, writing everything down. She looks up, her eyes revealing her thoughts. *Well, shit.*

"That's a big claim you're making. Can you tell me why you withheld this information yesterday at the station?" I ask.

"It wasn't anything sinister. Just a basic abortion, in Seattle." Jolie's tone is sharp, ready to slice us open. Her words are so contemporary but her clothing a costume. It makes it difficult to know if this is all a charade.

"And it's not our story to tell," Bernie says. "Kitty was doing what she thought was best. It isn't our business."

"What clinic was she going to?" I ask, frustrated that these girls have wasted so many hours of resources by holding back essential information. "We need to locate her. When was her appointment?"

"We don't know," Coretta says. "We don't have phones here, no internet. Good old Dunky sees to that."

"Dunky?" I ask.

"Duncan, the headmaster," Jolie fills in.

"She probably hitchhiked off the island, found a Planned Parenthood." Bernie's eyes fill with tears now, too. "She should be back by now."

"When was this?" Phoebe asks.

"She left Friday night," Diane says.

"Before or after Wells' accident?" I ask.

This causes the energy to shift. Bernie stops shuffling the cards in her hand. "After," she says, her voice cracking.

"And where were you, during the accident?"

"We were in the stables."

"You had been out with Wells? At night? Alone?"

The girls look away from Phoebe and me, eyes fixed on one another, silently willing something. Something deep and eternal, a secret not for me.

"So that's a yes," Phoebe says, groaning as she closes her notepad.

As we walk away from the girls, she sighs. "God, men really suck sometimes."

CHAPTER 17. WELLS

Freddy has been gone for hours. Tippy, annoyed with the lack of food in my house, went to the grocery store to gather provisions. Gin, mostly. She left wearing a pair of dark sunglasses and a bucket hat, as if she were going to be accosted by paparazzi. I don't remember the school year starting at Glennmare, but I do remember the population here is not the size of NYC.

Alone, I lie in my bed, eyes closed, willing my memories to return. It would all be so much easier if only I had the missing pieces to this story. Pieces that the detectives and headmaster need, now, in order to help find this missing girl.

A girl I seem to know intimately.

Before I can dwell any more on what all this means, there is a tapping on the bedroom window. Turning to look, I take in the faces of four young women, all startlingly beautiful.

"Wells?" the white-haired beauty whispers. "Can we come in?"

She is already raising the unlocked window, then helping lift a friend into my room, then another. Soon, they've all entered, sitting on my bed as if they've done this before. My stomach turns. How close was I to all these girls?

"You're looking at us like we're strangers," the redhead says, her eyes wide. "Do you really not know us?"

59

I run a hand through my hair, conscious of the fact I am a rumpled mess of a man. Wounded and left for dead — and I have no memory of any of it. I have felt the outsider many times in my life, but this is altogether different. This time I don't have the upper hand. This time, I am at everyone else's mercy.

"We met Freddy," says the one with dark eyes and straight, silky hair. "He was awful. I get why you had a falling out. You could never trust someone with eyes so twitchy."

I swallow, parched, and as if knowing my needs, one with dark brown hair hands me the glass of water on my bedside table.

"Thank you," I say, searching for her name.

"Bernadette," she says with a wide smile, rolling her R. "Everyone but you calls me Bernie."

"And Freddy and I . . . we're no longer friends?"

The girls look at me curiously. "No, not since October," the redhead says. "He wrote letters to you. I bet you saved them." She stands, looking around my room, pulling out the drawers in my dresser, riffling through my clothes.

The white-haired girl reaches for a leather satchel. "Maybe in here."

"Are we always this familiar?" I ask them.

They pause, all turning to look at me. The redhead smiles. "Not as familiar as you were with Kitty."

"Katherine?" I ask, my throat suddenly closing up. "Katherine Calloway? The missing girl?"

At this, the young women stop what they're doing, letters forgotten, tears filling their eyes. "He doesn't remember any of it!" Their voices fraught with anguish. "This is impossible." They pull up the window, ready to crawl out.

"Don't just leave. Help me. I want to remember. I want—"

"I don't know, Wells. Maybe you don't," Jolie says. "If you remember, it will change everything. And maybe . . . maybe ignorance is bliss."

"You can go back to before you met us, live in la-la land with Freddy and move back to Connecticut," Coretta adds.

"I hated my life there," I tell them. "I remember that much." I look at the girls. They are dressed so peculiarly; there is an innocence to their waistcoats and long plaid skirts, the bows at the neck of their blouses. "How old are you?"

Jolie smiles. "We're all eighteen. Kitty's the baby, but she's an adult now. We're all seniors."

Her words warm the chill in my bones. Even if I did do something inappropriate, it wasn't with a minor. There is some consolation in that, isn't there? The thought still leaves me feeling nauseated.

There is a noise from the front of the house. "Wells?" It's Freddy's booming voice.

Bernie reaches for my hand. "Let's meet at the old cabin. Turn left out your door and follow the path to the jetty, a half mile into the woods."

"When?"

"We'll let you know. If Kitty isn't back by tomorrow, we'll need to do something drastic."

The girls crawl out of the window just as Freddy opens my bedroom door.

"Damn, that draft is something fierce," he says jovially. "Oh shit, did I wake you?"

"No, I was already awake," I say, my gut in a knot. *I hate this man?* Can I trust the girls? I don't even know them — Freddy I've known for six years. Seven. "Tell me, Freddy, what sort of things did we discuss in the letters we wrote?"

He smiles, his arm leaning on my tall dresser. He eyes it curiously. "Looking for some clothes? Can I help locate something particular?"

"I was looking for a sweater, but I found it."

He looks at the mess. "When did you start leaving all your clothes lying around like this?"

"Things must have changed since I saw you last," I say, watching him closely for any hint of agreement.

"Time marches on," Freddy says.

"Look," I say, sitting up in bed. "I need to understand what has happened between us. This summer Tippy and I were fighting, you and I weren't speaking. Now you're both here. And I want to believe it's because we've all kissed and made up . . . but I feel like I'm missing something. Tell the truth, Freddy. You owe me that, at least."

Freddy paces the room, biting his nails. "I don't want to upset you while you're still recovering. Maybe a slower progression where your memories surface organically is better."

Irritated at being put off, I set my feet on the floor to stand, wanting to be face to face with this old friend of mine. "What aren't you saying?"

Freddy tugs at his hair, clearly conflicted. "We did fight once you moved here. Things with Tippy didn't end after you left . . ." His face falls. "I kept . . ."

I scoff, aghast, and yet, why am I surprised? Freddy was always devoted to Tippy. "You kept sleeping with her?"

He clenches his jaw. "It's over. That's why she was so pissed at Christmas. I cut her off."

I look at him, wondering if it is possible to stop loving someone who has a portion of your heart. I don't feel hate toward him if the worst of it is an affair. I'd hate him more if he wasn't wearing his heart on his sleeve, telling it to me straight.

"Why didn't I forgive you?" I ask him.

"You were distracted, utterly obsessed with this place, with Glennmare. It had a hold on you from the start and, honestly, I didn't want to pull you back to the past when it seemed as if you were determined to move forward."

"I can see being in love with this place. The sea's like nothing I've ever seen before." I look out my bedroom window that the young women just climbed through. "The students from my seminar seem particularly attached to me."

He nods slowly. "About them. I met those girls."

"And?"

"I don't trust them. They seem . . . they seem to be very close to you." He pauses, weighing his words. "And I wouldn't want an allegation to injure your future."

"What are you implying?"

Freddy groans, pacing my room. "Remember how you slept with that student when you were a teacher's aide, a few years back?"

I clench my jaw, hand on my broken ribs. "I remember. Iris. And the fact she was a student was a technicality."

"Well, technically speaking, you could have been fired, or worse, Wells."

"What does Iris have to do with anything now? That was ages ago."

"She was a freshman, you were twenty-four, and you were in a position of power. I just wonder . . . if it might be a pattern."

"You're suggesting I slept with these students? You have some nerve, Frederick. We were barely on speaking terms this summer, completely fell out this fall, and now you come here suggesting . . ." I shake my head, appalled.

"I didn't *want* you to remember this fall, Wells. We fought. A lot. And then, we parted ways."

"I hate that we fought so much."

Freddy shakes his head. "Well, I hate that you broke Tippy's heart."

"Can't we separate anything?"

"She's my sister!"

"For the record, you have only got her side of things about what happened this summer. We never talked about it, you and me."

"That isn't true. We wrote about it, *you* wrote me about it," Freddy says emphatically. "You said that this summer she refused to be in a relationship with you, and you were angry. You lashed out at her. It is a wonder she is here at all, serving you, Wells. You scared her."

I shake my head, exhausted. Maybe he was right: hashing this out isn't making me feel any better. "I remember the fight with Tippy, on the Fourth of July, and there was no lashing. It was two adults finally telling the truth. We wanted different things."

"What did you want, Wells?"

63

"Tippy didn't want me. So I wanted to move on. It's why I came here. But I still don't understand what Tippy and I have to do with you."

"It was more than the Fourth of July, Wells." Freddy scoffs, his irritation palpable. "You and Tippy . . . it was bigger than a singular fight. I know you haven't forgotten that."

I swallow, wanting to ignore the parts I remember. Sleeping together in secret for months, behind Freddy's back.

Pushing the heat off me, I remind him of these claims of his. "And somehow, you've decided that in the time since you saw me last, I went on a bender sleeping with students?" I scoff, horrified. "It's really quite the allegation."

"Don't look at me like that," Freddy says. "I met the students in your seminar. They aren't like other girls."

I know he is right about that. They were in my room for five minutes and dismantled everything I thought. *Meet at a cabin. Not as familiar as you were with Kitty.*

The front door opens. "I made it back in one piece," Tippy sings.

Freddy smirks. "Lovely timing."

"Are you going to tell her your theories about me?"

He shakes his head. "I'm sure she has theories of her own about you, Wells. But you're my best friend, whatever happened this fall."

"The months I can't remember?"

He nods.

I look Freddy over, this man who has been like a brother to me, who holds cards I can't yet see. But his intentions seem pure. He has always been so good to me.

He bought me a horse and saddle, so when I visited his family's country estate I could ride. He let me live there, on every school break, for years. Without asking for anything in return. He just gave and gave and gave. Even when he learned my origin story was a farce, even when he should have looked at me with shame, Freddy was there. Tippy was there too, until she wasn't.

"I hope your theory isn't true," I tell him, standing from my bed.

Freddy places a hand on my shoulder. "If it is, you won't get through it alone. The past is just that, the past. I'm here now."

CHAPTER 18. JOHANNA

The dining hall is full of students as I carry in platters of roast chicken and vegetables, fresh rolls and carafes of milk. The food is shared family-style, here at Glennmare, and that is just one of the reasons I fell in love with this place.

After losing Matilda, I was so lonely. I needed a change. And my basement apartment depressed me every time I entered it. The only way to get out of that dark depression was to change my life completely.

So I searched the internet: *cook for hire with lodging*. I found myself with plenty of positions to consider. But Glennmare was my first choice. No one could find me here — they don't even have a website. I found a posting for the position on a job site and was intrigued when I saw Glennmare's location. Far enough away that I could start over. No one would be ringing me up asking how I was holding up.

I could start over, which is what I did.

And Lord, did I get lucky. My room is adjacent to the kitchen and has a huge window, a full bed, a private bathroom, even. And being next to the kitchen means whenever any students come in for a late-night snack, raiding the pantry after having a little too much fun with the booze or pot, I can listen in.

Not to eavesdrop but to make sure they are all safe. All okay. That no one is in serious trouble.

Which is how I came upon Kitty a week ago.

She was alone — which was unusual in and of itself. She was always with her roommates — Jolie, Coretta, Bernie and Diane. Always. They moved as one, all eyes on Wells Halifax.

Now, I am not one to judge, but that man was intent on wrapping every single student in his classes around his finger. He did it in a matter of weeks.

Though, to be fair, it wouldn't take much for these girls, who are so starved for male attention. I told the headmaster he shouldn't even hire male teachers, that these girls have raging hormones and can't handle the temptation, but he thought my fears were hogwash. He insisted Halifax had glowing recommendations and was going to be an asset.

That night last week, Kitty was in the kitchen, late at night, crying into the leftover lasagna from last night's dinner. I took the ceramic dish from her hand, warmed it up on the stove while she told me her troubles.

"I'm pregnant," she whispered. "And I can't tell my parents. They hate me already."

I sat across from her, topping the pasta with parmesan and pouring her a big glass of whole milk, inwardly beaming that she chose me to be her confidante. I always knew the girls trusted me; this just proved it.

"What do you want to do, Kitty? You have options, you know."

"I can't have a child," she said, as if it was obvious. "I turned eighteen two months ago. I'm going to Yale next year. I can't be a mother, not now."

"So what do you want to do?"

Kitty shoveled the pasta into her pink mouth, her eyes glassy, her shiny brown hair loose around her face, her nightgown nearly falling from her narrow shoulders. If I were to line the five girls up and choose who was the loveliest, I would pick Kitty every time. She is beautiful, but that's the least interesting thing about her.

She is outgoing and sincere, the most devoted to the friend group. She coordinates parties for everyone's birthdays, comes out to the kitchen to bake cakes when someone has done exceptionally well in an assignment, she paints her friends' nails, and if someone has drunk too much, she holds back their hair.

I only know this because it is my job to observe. Technically my job is to cook, but as I set down their food on the long wooden tables in the dining hall I catch tidbits of conversation, gather the group dynamics. And not just of this fivesome, of all the students at Glennmare.

Which is why it was so odd to see Kitty without her friends that night in the kitchen.

"I need to go to a clinic. Soon. Before . . . well, just soon."

"Do you need help driving there?" I asked.

She furrowed her brow. "No. I can manage. I just need money."

None of the girls here have much spending money, only small sums of petty cash. Their devices and wallets are handed over to the headmaster upon arrival and without several hundreds of dollars, she couldn't exactly get this procedure done.

"I can help," I told her. "I have money."

Her eyes widened. "You'd do that, for me?"

"Of course, love." I patted her hand, thinking that my Matilda would have opened up to me this way too, if she needed help.

"Do you have it now?" she asked, wiping her eyes.

I frowned, not expecting to be put on the spot like this.

She shook her head. "Never mind, I shouldn't have asked you. This is embarrassing."

"No," I rushed to say, wanting to help her more than she understood. "I have it in my room. Give me one minute."

I walked to my bedroom and reached for the box in the back of my closet, pulling out ten one-hundred-dollar bills. That should be plenty. Get her there, and back, safely. She could hire a car both ways. As I walked back in the kitchen, I made a suggestion. "I can take you myself."

She shook her head. "No, that would raise too many questions. I just need to do this without anyone noticing."

She looked at the cash in my palm.

I handed it over. "If you want to talk about the person who did this to you, if you need to—"

She stepped back. "Oh God, no. No one did anything to me. I wanted this. Well, I wanted *that*, not *this*," she says with an unexpected laugh, pressing a hand to her belly. "Anyways, thank you so much, this means the world to me. I will repay you as soon as I can get my credit card back from Dunky."

"Don't even think about it," I told her as she rushed out of the kitchen, not looking back. A teenager, I thought. One who hasn't yet learned proper manners.

* * *

Now, as I carry plates of oatmeal raisin cookies into the dining hall for the girls' dessert after their chicken, I notice the roommates, sans Kitty. They look over at me, smiling.

But now I have an uncomfortable inkling that maybe they aren't smiling at all.

Maybe they are laughing.

CHAPTER 19. DETECTIVE PHOEBE BAKER

When I moved to Whidbey Island, from Seattle, I had one goal in mind: Get the hell away from my ex.

That was three years ago. Before moving here, I never knew a good man. You may think that's me being a drama queen, but it's the truth. My father was never in my life, my grandad was dead before I was born — and my radar was off when it came to men. Way off. Like, only choose the guys who hurt me, off.

Then I meet Leonard — my partner here on the island — and suddenly I'm getting all close and personal with this old teddy bear who is a little closed-minded but a lot big-hearted, and, honestly, I needed to meet a man like him in order to believe not all guys are dicks.

After coming across a handful of men I don't particularly care for this morning — the headmaster, Wells Halifax, and Frederick Rooper — I am more grateful than ever to have a decent guy at my side during the workday.

Leaving Glennmare Academy, me behind the wheel, him in the passenger seat, I feel an immense sense of relief.

I somehow escaped the hellscape of being a teenage girl and am on the other side.

"Was the school what you imagined?" Leonard asks.

"Shouldn't I be asking you that? I've never met a girl from Glennmare before today. You've done more than meet one."

"And what do you think now? Was my assessment right?"

"Too early to tell."

Leonard buckles up and I pull out of the parking lot, heading to the station to interview the guy who admitted he bought booze for Kitty. "Katherine was sleeping with her teacher then left to get an abortion. Hell, that's more answers than we were expecting to get."

"We don't know if either of those things are true," I say, scowling. "The friends could be lying through their teeth. When you're a teenage girl there's nothing you won't do for your friends. That includes deceiving the police."

Leonard looks out the window, alarmed. "Does that mean Cassidy could be lying to me about something?"

"Probably. She's sixteen. But don't worry too much — it's a rite of passage to sneak behind your parent's back."

"If Wells really did do something with the girls while they were alone, if he slept with Katherine . . . it's more than sneaking around. It's trouble for him," Leonard says. "She was his student."

"If that is true."

"Why don't you believe it?"

"I'm not saying I don't, I would just like it confirmed by the person in question, not her friends who are in varying states of distress."

Leonard looks over at me, perplexed. "I thought we are supposed to believe women when they say they've been—"

I cut him off. "First of all, don't get all *me too* at me as if I'm some sort of idiot. I understand more than anyone that you need to believe a woman when they tell you they've been assaulted." I unroll my window, suddenly hot and agitated. "That isn't what we're dealing with here. Not yet at least. All we know is some students think Katherine left Friday night, around ten p.m., to get an abortion. That's all we know right now. We have no confirmation that Wells Halifax had anything to do with that situation. It's all hearsay." My grip on the wheel is tight, my shoulders tensed.

"Damn, okay, I wasn't trying to upset you."

I groan. "Whatever."

"Did I say something?" Leonard asks.

Tears sting my eyes. Memories I don't want to relive. "It's nothing," I lie, the truth tight in my chest.

"Pull over."

When I choose to accelerate instead, Leonard gets uncharacteristically loud. "Dammit, Phoebe, I mean it."

I do as he says, pulling into a turnoff, taking the keys out of the ignition.

"Talk to me," he presses.

"He could have slept with her. Or slept with all of them. He is appealing, even with his pathetic ribs broken. And I would have fallen for that act. Hell, I probably still would if given the chance."

"What do you mean?" Leonard asks. "Not trying to sound like a fucking idiot, but what are you talking about?"

I blow my nose. He winces.

"What I mean is men like Wells Halifax have this ability to make a woman feel seen."

"He did that to you?"

I shake my head. "No, we didn't meet in that context. But I could tell. Hell, both those best friends of his, Freddy and Tippy, are at his beck and call. The girls were anxious and all worked up about wanting to please him. Even the headmaster thinks the world of Halifax."

"Which makes him suspicious?"

"Yes. Especially if he knows where Kitty is."

"You realize a few minutes ago you were telling me I was wrong to assume anything about Wells Halifax?"

I close my eyes, dropping my forehead to the wheel. "I don't know what to think. We need proof of something."

"When you said you knew more than other women, what did you mean?"

I look over at Leonard, the best man I know. If I am going to be honest with anyone, I choose him. "My ex, he was . . . bad. He forced me against my will. A lot. Raped me, if we're being blunt. Made me feel small in ways I wasn't. It's why I went to the police academy. I never wanted to feel that way again."

The skin around Leonard's eyes creases, and he sets his big hand on top of mine where it rests on the gear shift. "You're a good cop, Phoebe. And that ex of yours, I hope he paid for what he did to you."

"You're a detective, you know it's not so simple as that. Sometimes the good guys lose and the bad guys win."

"He was never charged?" Leonard asks.

I shake my head. "I got hired here as an officer and left town, for good."

"You deserve so much more than what you got. You know that, Phoebe, don't you?"

I smile over at Leonard. He is imperfect, sure, has biases, clearly — but he knows what side of the story is the right one.

"We need to find out if Wells is a felon or just a guy who fell off a horse," I say.

"That your way of telling me to stop being so damn sappy?"

I shake my head as I take the keys and start the car. "No. It's my way of saying thank you for not being like the rest."

CHAPTER 20. THE GIRLS

We leave the dining hall with oatmeal cookies in our hands, not wanting that creeper Johanna to look at us one more time. It's awkward, the way she is always listening in. Depressing too. She really thinks Kitty is her friend or something. Probably the same way Eli thought he was Kitty's friend.

Back in the room, we lie on our beds, curtains open, staring at the swollen moon. We have no homework and tomorrow is Monday. A new week, a new beginning. Except everything feels off.

"I hate that Dunky put him on leave. Who do you think will be teaching our seminar tomorrow?" Coretta asks.

"I'm not going," Bernie says. "I'll call my parents and tell them I'm ill if the nurse makes a fuss. I need a mental health day. We all do."

Diane hasn't stopped crying. "I shouldn't have broken like that. The detective wasn't even pressing me."

"What's done is done. Now we can move on. Think about meeting at the cabin. We should do it tomorrow night," Jolie says, sitting behind Diane, wrapping an arm around her.

"You think Kitty will still be gone? Will Wells even show up at the cabin?" Coretta asks.

"He won't come if he remembers what happened last time," Bernie says, her voice hushed, the memories from Friday night fresh in her mind. Did we really do all that? Did he?

It wasn't Wells Halifax's idea. He wouldn't tell it like that, but we all would.

When we arrived in his Irish Lit seminar, we were ready for him to impart his wisdom upon us. With lined paper and pencils sharp enough to stab, we were eager. Giddy. We'd seen the new teacher around campus. But mostly, we saw him on the horses.

And God, can that man ride.

We joined the school a year ago, or longer; none of us transferred in for the new semester. We were roommates, soulmates, and didn't care if that sounded juvenile. Best friends forever, pinky promises, blood sisters. If you can be in a committed long-term relationship with your best friends — we were.

We knew the ropes to Glennmare. Write longer answers than required if you want an A. They threaten to call home but rarely do. The boys from Oak Harbor who party at the beach are always willing.

We also knew one another intimately by then. We knew Jolie is the outcast daughter of a governor. We knew Coretta has an evil stepmother and a nice grandma and that once when she went home for a break her dad beat her up. We knew Bernie had been in several treatment centers before here but that she's curbed her pill habit and that we're her saving grace. We knew Diane is the daughter of a super-model and an actor, and that when she was little they were Scientologists. We knew Kitty's good-girl act was just that — an act. She was more of a saber tooth, but her jealous streak wasn't something any of us knew about then.

At Glennmare we had no TV, no iPad, no email. We were obsessed with one another because we were all we had.

Diane won't eat after seven p.m. and Jolie slashes her thighs with razor blades, which is better than what she used to cut, and Bernie got a nose job for her sixteenth birthday and Kitty said her first orgasm was given by Wells, and Coretta throws up the candy her grandmother sends her, and together that might seem like a lot but truly it isn't. We are just girls, clinging to one another. Wild and crazed, loathing everything we haven't yet become.

We also knew all those secrets of ours were kept by Kitty — with a threat. If we didn't play by her rules, she was willing to use them against us.

"If you really love me, you won't break my heart," she whispered in our room, cupping our cheeks, her eyes locked on ours. "And best friends aren't heartbreakers, are they?"

Of course not, we promised.

We never said no to her until it was too late.

So when we started classes in the fall, the seminar with Mr. Halifax felt like the promise of something new.

We weren't wrong.

That first day Kitty set an apple on his desk, and we sat in a circle, him too, and he reached for that apple and took bite after bite until it was gone and juice dripped down his chin and he tossed the core in the bin and we were done for. All of us, even Jolie.

We were a captive audience and Wells was better than any television show we'd ever seen. We couldn't look away.

He was young and wore wrinkled suits and a hidden smile and his black hair was long and his eyes were too dark and he offered up his soul to us in every lecture.

How did he do that? It was simple. He read us stories and asked us questions. Ones no one ever asked before.

What do you think?
How does that make you feel?
What is the pain in that paragraph?
What does this stir within you?

We were mesmerized. Irish Literature could have been anything. It could have been Polish or Portuguese. For us, all that mattered was Mr. Halifax reciting poetry and reading stanzas, and then following it up, every single time, by asking us what we thought.

What we thought.

Not what he wanted us to think. Not what we were taught to say. Not what we were supposed to believe.

He skipped past all the bullshit that first day when he ate his apple, then asked us, point-blank, what we loved most in the world.

Coretta said her grandma.

Diane said the ocean.

Jolie said giving cunnilingus.

We all laughed at that; Wells' eyebrows raised.

Bernie said tarot cards.

Kitty said risks.

"What do you mean, risks?" Wells Halifax asked.

Kitty tucked her long brown hair behind her ears, her upturned nose cute as a button. "I love the thrill that comes with danger."

"You don't get scared?" Wells asked her.

Kitty shook her head. "Never."

We didn't believe her, because we knew about Eli, who cornered her one night after she asked him to buy her liquor.

She had cried throughout her explanation of what had transpired. "He was awful, I wasn't sure I would get away."

"Should we tell the headmaster?" we asked, horrified with her account of the assault.

Eli hurt Kitty, and we didn't want to stand by without speaking up. Eli wasn't a local highschooler. He was from out of town. We knew nothing about him. But that didn't mean he wouldn't be back. She made us swear we wouldn't say a thing.

By then we knew not to betray her trust.

Wells cleared his throat, in the classroom, then smiled at all of us before reaching for his notebook in his leather messenger bag.

"What about you?" Kitty asked. "What do you love most?"

"Pushing boundaries," he said with a wink to us all.

That's when we knew he was going to teach us everything we wanted to know.

"This seminar is on early Irish literature," he told us. "It is my area of expertise, and soon it will be yours."

We diligently took notes, even Jolie, and in the afternoons we would lie on the lawn, discussing what it would have been like to live five hundred years ago in Ireland. We laughed, thinking in some ways it wasn't so different than what we experienced now. No technology, and often no heat; we rode horses instead of cars.

Kitty was most eager to please Wells, though at first she was too enamored to say as much out loud. She spent extra hours in the school library, wanting to bring something new and interesting to the discussions.

We began to quote pagan sagas and poetry. Coretta would cradle Bernie's face and speak dramatically as we got ready for bed at night. *"O lady fair, wouldst thou come with me, to the wondrous land that is ours?"*

Jolie would light a joint, sitting on the sill of the open window, and speak to everyone and no one, reciting verses. *"None now learn a song to sing, For long our fern is fading."*

The next few weeks were a blur. We'd show up in class, eager for more. We never cared so much about learning before, but things shifted inside us. We were happy, settled; inspired, even.

For all our lives we had been the mistakes and the misfits and the misguided. Now, to Wells Halifax at least, we were scholars.

Seminars became more casual. One fall day, the leaves a magnificent burnt orange, he suggested we ride horses in lieu of sitting in the classroom. We went to the stables, each saddling our favorite horse.

Kitty spoke up. "Have you ever heard of the Knight's Rite?"

Wells looked over at her, frowning. "Sure. I take it so have you?"

She nodded as she climbed onto her horse.

"I'm surprised you have. It's very obscure," Wells added.

We watched as she began to ride beside our teacher. Her eyes had a glint in them. "Pretty demented, right?"

We asked them to describe it.

"In Ireland," Wells explained, "horse sacrifice was part of an inauguration rite. The Irish ritual was chronicled by Giraldus Cambrensis in 1185 AD."

"What did it entail?" Coretta asked. "Please tell me they didn't hurt any horses."

"It is unseemly, Coretta — maybe you'd better ride ahead," Wells said.

"No, I want to know," she said.

"They would appoint a king," Wells explained. "But he first had to perform the rite, to prove his sovereignty. Horses have long been linked to the holy realm, and so being bound to a horse was as if being bound to God."

"I don't get it," Jolie said. "What do you mean, bound?"

"Well, some Indo-European clans would quite literally require a king to become one with a horse," Wells said.

"Like bestiality? Sick, Kitty. Why are you reading that?"

"That isn't what the Knight's Rite was, exactly," she said, piqued.

"You're right." Wells smirked, looking at Kitty with sparks of light in his eyes, as if her mind was something to behold. "It's worse."

Kitty glowed from his attention, and it spurred her on to keep talking, "All the people in town or whatever would gather, and a white mare would be brought forward—"

Bernie groaned. "Please don't tell me the king fucks the horse. I'm gonna be sick."

"Well, actually," Kitty said, matter-of-factly. "Yes. He has intercourse with the horse and then tells everyone he's a beast too. Then they sacrifice the mare immediately."

"Oh God, Kitty, stop," Diane said, pulling her horse to a stop and petting its mane. She leaned down, resting her head against it.

"They butcher the mare and boil it in water and then the new king serves everyone the meat."

"That's very unsanitary." Bernie scowled. "Also very weird."

"It was a different time," Kitty said. "I've been reading all these pieces that are a thousand years old — they were simply practicing their beliefs, which were normal at the time."

"Are you saying it was okay to sacrifice horses?" Bernie asked. "Because I love you, Kitty-Cat, but that's disturbing."

Kitty was undeterred. "They thought it brought them closer to God. Wouldn't you do anything to be closer to the unknown?"

Wells got off his horse then, and we all followed suit. We were at the old cabin on the edge of Glennmare's property.

"That's a good question," he said. "How far would you go for a deeper understanding? For truth? For love?"

He looked at Kitty then and we all simultaneously swooned because there was something there, between them, and we all felt their growing devotion. We all saw it unfold in real time. We all believed.

Kitty walked toward Wells then, the rest of us entranced as she wrapped her arms around his neck, as she looked adoringly into his eyes.

Nothing like this ever happened before. We watched, stunned, but captivated. It was as if Kitty truly could have anything she wanted, and her arms around our teacher was proof of that.

Wells was still, his eyes zeroed in on Kitty, and our hearts pounded, wanting more. Wanting it all.

All semester we'd been reading about maidens married at fourteen and women sold to men twice their age and so this — this relationship that was developing before our eyes — was not complicated. It was what we all desired.

"There are many phases of this ritual," Wells said as we tied our horses to trees and entered the derelict cabin. "The sexual act, the sacrifice and the eating of food. The rite signified two things: the universal cycle of the fertility process and the sovereignty the king had over his people and land."

Inside the cabin we unpacked our lunches from our bags. Cheese and pears and almonds.

"It's beautiful, really," Kitty said as she nibbled the fruit.

Diane nodded slowly. "I can see how the idea of a king that would do anything for his people, even degrade himself, could be intriguing . . . but there has to be limits to what we call beauty. Slaughtering an innocent animal isn't beautiful. It's horrifying."

"It's so twisted. Can you imagine someone doing *anything* for you? Just to prove their loyalty?" Jolie asked in an unexpected moment of sincerity. "To fuck and kill and give everything for your happiness?"

"You don't think the king liked it?" Bernie asked skeptically. "The power, the control?"

"Maybe," Coretta said. "But it was a different time. We can't even imagine what it was like back then. Maybe this wasn't weird. Maybe it was normal."

"It's horse sex!" Bernie shook her head, pulling her tarot cards from her bag and shuffling them, as was her habit when she was nervous. "You've lost your minds if you think this is anything more than a perverse ritual."

"What do you think, Wells?" Kitty asked our teacher. They were sitting side by side, the sexual tension unmistakable.

"I think that being devoted to someone, or something, can look different for everyone. Judging an ancient rite when we were not there, in those times, feels impossible. The concept of right and wrong changes in every context."

"So you'd sleep with a horse?" Bernie asked, not having any of it.

"Of course not," Wells said, aghast. "I'm merely saying the people who participated in this rite were doing so with the belief that it would make their lives better, not worse."

"So is there such a thing as right and wrong?" Coretta asked, looking at the fingers of her dear friend and the beloved teacher.

Kitty looked past us, through the open cabin doors, to the sea in the distance, the wild island woods crawling through the worn floorboards and broken windows.

"Not for girls like us," she said. "We were sent away. And now? Now we are free."

CHAPTER 21. FREDDY

In the morning, I take another walk, needing to collect my thoughts. Rationalize my fears. I find myself in the stables, though I haven't ridden in years.

"Oh." A voice pulls me from my introspection. "Do you need something?"

It's Bernie, one of Wells' girls. I immediately reject that phrase. Wells has no girls. He is a grown man, a teacher, and these are simply his students.

"I don't need anything, just wanted to see the horses that Wells loves so much."

Bernie nods but doesn't offer a smile. "He rode every day. Says he learned to ride from his uncle, in Appalachia, where he grew up."

Now it's my turn to nod, even though her statement is wholly false. I don't dispute Bernie's understanding of our dear friend Wells. We all have interpretations of the truth, and his story is not mine to tell.

"Which horse is his favorite?" I ask her. She's leaning against a horse stall, shuffling a deck of tarot cards in her hands absently.

"It was the white mare." She exhales slowly. "But she isn't here anymore."

"Where did she go?"

Bernie blinks, her eyes glassy. "It doesn't matter."

Sensing there is plenty more to this story, I try a different approach. "My sister liked tarot cards when she was a teenager, too."

Bernie smirks. "Sure she did. Don't all girls? We want to be witches because we know the world won't give us power. We have to take it."

"Pretty grim outlook."

"Says the man who is the son of a millionaire."

"You know a lot about me, then?" I pull out my cigarettes and offer her one.

"Enough." Bernie accepts.

I pause. "Oh fuck, you're a student. I can't give you a cigarette. Or say fuck in front of you. Dammit."

She smirks. "I'm eighteen. And believe me, I smoke more than tobacco. I think you're fine."

"Aren't there rules about not smoking on campus?"

Bernie shakes her head. "Nothing like that is enforced. The teachers want us to be engaged in the learning process more than anything."

Taking her words at face value, I light hers, then mine, with my father's lighter. I am not on staff here and Bernie is an adult. "So Wells told you about me?"

Bernie inhales, and we exit the cabin, turning right, toward the rocky shore. "Wells likes to talk, hold court."

"And what do you think of that?"

"Are you a detective now?"

"No, I'm simply trying to piece together the last few months of my friend's life. Seems like there is more to it than a man getting tossed from a horse."

"He's a good teacher, I mean that. I've never been taken so seriously by anyone in my life. I'm not his favorite, but it doesn't matter. He respects me."

"And do you respect him?"

Bernie flicks the ash, arms crossed. She looks at me with sympathy. "I love him. Not like that, but, like, I would do anything for him."

"You didn't answer the question. Do you respect him?"

"He would ask me for tarot readings and I liked that." Bernie smiles at the memory. "His interest. Love is when you learn what brings the other person joy, just to know them better. Even if you don't like it."

"Wells didn't like the readings?"

Bernie laughs. "Not mine. I always forget the meaning of the cards I pull or what it means when something is reversed. That's why he started going to see Marjorie — she knows everything about tarot and you know Wells, he loves to learn, especially things that are obscure."

"Marjorie, is she local?"

Bernie nods. "Yeah, she has a shop in Coupeville. Downtown. Marjorie's Magik."

I have a hard time imagining Wells going to a tarot reader, but it seems there are plenty of things I don't know about my friend.

Stomping my cigarette, I thank Bernie for the chat.

"You know," I add. "Witches are one of the only forms of female empowerment that don't derive their power from men."

She looks at me, pityingly. "Why the hell do you think I carry this deck around with me?"

I walk away, having the rare sensation of being like Glennmare's Headmaster Dunky, wondering if this is a feeling I should have more often.

Being more wrong than right.

CHAPTER 22. WELLS

Tippy brings me a new dosage of medicine, sitting on the edge of my bed. She looks well rested, at peace, as if the island air is doing her well. And her choice to be here now, in my time of need, after everything, is something I will never forget.

"You have to drink this water," she tells me.

I do as she asks. She lifts my shirt and winces at my wounds. "I need to change these bandages again."

I nod. "Thank you," I say. "For being here."

"Of course." She cares for my wounds silently. When finished, she asks if I want to move to the living room. "Maybe we could talk? I think it's overdue."

I follow her to the small living room, my mind not on Tippy and Freddy at all. My mind caught up in my dreams. Ever since the girls came to my window yesterday, I can't help seeing them every time I close my eyes.

"What is it?" she asks. She wears a pair of black slacks and a white button-down shirt, classic, timeless.

"I wish I had my memories back," I tell her. "I know how things ended between us, in the summer. It was bad, Tippy. And now you're here, like it didn't happen."

"We mended things this fall," she says quietly. "I wish you could remember."

"And Freddy, is that over?"

She blanches. "God, yes. Long over. Though he won't forgive me."

"He will in time." I lean back on the couch, tired from walking out here. "He forgave me, all those years ago. Same as you."

Tippy's face softens. "We're all just trying to survive. We do it in different ways, right?"

Our freshman year at Yale, I spun an origin story of me and my uncle in the Appalachian Mountains. I told them I was a scholarship student, with no family. They took me under their wing and protected me. They devoted themselves to me, both of them, as if I were their project. I loved it. The attention, the constant need. The unyielding friendship.

When winter break came around at the end of the first term, they asked where I was going. I admitted I planned on staying in the dorms, not realizing they were closing. Freddy immediately asked me to join them at their family home.

"I can't impose," I said, secretly grateful for the chance to see their Manhattan lifestyle.

It was decadent, all three weeks. We skated at Rockefeller Center and looked at the holiday displays in shop windows. On Christmas morning Tippy gave me a cashmere sweater and Freddy gave me a proper watch. I gifted Freddy a watercolor painting of his favorite tree on campus and Tippy a book, inscribing it with the words, *We'll always have poetry.*

At dinner, their parents asked about my family. They'd hardly been around all break. Now, I was face to face with them, eating their Baron of Beef and sipping their sherry.

Tippy jumped in, explaining my uncle, the mountains, the fact I was all alone.

Her mother pressed a hand to her chest. Freddy's father shook his head. "You've done fine for yourself, son, getting to Yale."

I knew the comment hurt Freddy. His father had withheld compliments from his son all his life. And there I was lying through my teeth, receiving their kindness.

I had to come clean.

After dinner, utterly drunk and entirely full, the three of us sat smoking on the back patio of the mansion. It was snowing and we were bundled in winter coats and hats, passing a bottle of wine.

"I have to confess," I told them in an act of alcohol-induced bravery. I knew it might cost me everything. But I loved them both so much that I knew telling the truth would be the only way I could continue without wanting to literally kill myself. Telling the truth would mean I wasn't all bad.

"When we met this fall, and I told you about where I grew up, it wasn't true."

Freddy frowned, looking at me. "Whatever do you mean?"

"I am from Indiana, the Midwest, the heartland. My parents are alive, and I have an older brother named Vincent who is in the Marines."

"What are you talking about?" Tippy shook her head. "You . . . made the orphan thing up?"

"I learned to ride horses at my uncle's ranch. But he has a rambler, not a trailer. But my parents might as well be dead to me."

"Wells!" Tippy shook her head. "Don't say that. My father really is dead. God! What is the matter with you?"

Tears filled my eyes and I dropped my head in my hands, shoulders shaking. "I'm sorry. I didn't know we were going to be friends. I was rambling about this character I was writing about in a novel, and acting as if I was him, and, yes, that is mental, but God, I never thought we'd become . . . that we'd be . . ."

"Best of friends?" Freddy asked.

I lifted my eyes to meet his. "Exactly. I am an idiot, I know that, but dammit, I love you both so much and I had to come clean. If you can forgive me, please do, and if you can't, I will leave tonight."

"To where?" Freddy asked, aghast. "A bus to Indiana? Wells, don't be absurd."

I wiped my eyes. "I've ruined Christmas Day and—"

"You haven't ruined anything." Tippy took a slug of wine, wiped her mouth. "We've never had a Christmas dinner that pleasant, ever. You are the thread that is holding this entire break together. You can't go now. Not ever."

"A bit protective, are you?" Freddy teased his stepsister.

"He may be a lying piece of shit, but he's one of us." Tippy turns to me, suddenly somber. "You know that, right, Wells?" She shoved my arm, suddenly playful. Letting me off the hook.

I got down on my knees, kneeling before them both. "Forgive me, please."

I left home because my parents never really wanted me — I wasn't an athlete like my brother, a cowboy like my uncle. I was always reading or writing, which wasn't of any interest to my parents. I wanted them to love me, accept me as I was — but I learned early on that was never, ever going to happen. That was my motivation to leave, to find people who might truly appreciate me and accept me as I was.

I had to come clean that winter night. I wanted my two dearest friends in all the world to see me as I was and love me because of that. It was a risk — one I felt necessary to take.

It paid off. My confession meant I was more loyal than ever.

"Fine," Freddy said. "But you must never lie to us again."

"I swear it." I picked Tippy up by the waist and carried her to the backyard, dropping her in the snow like an angel. She pulled me to her, I leaned over her narrow frame, our noses touched. I could have kissed her.

I rolled over and Freddy flopped down by my side, and the three of us looked up at the snowy night sky. I reached for both their hands, and we held still.

"I'm sorry," I whispered. "For not being what you wanted me to be."

"It's better like this," Freddy said. "Besides, you were too sympathetic, being both an orphan and at Yale on scholarship. It made us look bad, how perfect you were."

I laughed, and so did they. And I knew then that no matter how messed up life became, these two were my family.

Tippy sits next to me now, in the cottage at Glennmare Academy, waiting to talk.

But I don't want to talk right now. Because, somehow, we went from being snow angels to drifting so far apart.

"What are you thinking?" she asks.

"Until I remember everything, I don't want to discuss where our friendship went wrong or how we made it right."

Tippy nods, blinking back tears. "Fine. But, Wells, we were more than friends."

I swallow, knowing I could never forget that fact.

CHAPTER 23. TIPPY

Freddy left for a walk, Wells won't talk and I need some distance.

In my rental car, I drive away from Glennmare, north, to Deception Pass. It's a state park with a narrow bridge dividing the island from the mainland. Beneath it there is a rocky shore and dark, perilous waters. The pass got its name for a reason. I park my car and get out, realizing that a Monday morning in February isn't exactly a prime time to visit the beauty spot. The lot is nearly empty.

Thankfully I am wearing leather boots and as I pull on my gloves, breath clouds in front of me as I fill my lungs deeply.

I walk the jagged path, past the massive rocks hugging the shore and the prehistoric-looking, waist-high ferns. No one is out here tonight; it's cold and windy, but I want to feel the icy air on my face, clearing my mind. It's impossible not to wish things were different. With the boys, but also life. It wasn't supposed to be like this.

I pause, sitting on a large piece of pale beach wood, wishing I had a cigarettes. My entire body is itching for relief as I think about what brought me here — Wells. And how it was all going to play out differently in my mind. I thought

I'd simply nurse him back to health and he would look at me like he used to and Freddy wouldn't be jealous. So jealous, all the time. It wasn't my fault our parents were married — or that I could never love him back the way he needed me to.

He doesn't care about that. Freddy will forever be mad he took second place.

Climbing up the steep hill, I reach the enormous bridge. I begin to walk across it, trucks and cars zooming past me. I wrap my hands around the railing, looking over the edge at the great expanse of dark water below.

What it would be to simply fall. To be free.

I shouldn't be here. I need to go back to the cottage, check on Wells. If his memory returns while I'm gone, and he's all alone, facing the facts — it would be too much.

I begin to walk back to my car, not at all settled. In the parking lot, standing near the restrooms, a woman in a black raincoat smiles at me. "Hi," she says warmly. "Didn't think we'd meet again."

I return the smile, having no idea who she is. I swear this island is way too small for my tastes. I need to get back to Manhattan, stat.

She is stapling something to the bulletin board under the covered area. I glance at it. A missing person flier. "It's my roommate's cousin. He was always camping in the area, in his van. No one has heard from him for a week."

"Hope it's all okay," I say, not wanting to engage with this woman I don't know.

"Thanks." She returns to her stapling and I cross the parking lot.

When I reach my car, I see I have reception and immediately check my messages. My friend from my old MFA program, Tanya, is asking if I can meet for a new gallery opening a week from now. Luc, my hairdresser's assistant, is calling to confirm a booking for later this week. I was supposed to be home from my writing retreat by now, and without service at Glennmare I haven't exactly been able to keep people up to speed on my life.

I type out quick texts, punctuated by kissy face emojis, knowing they would make Freddy puke and Wells smile.

Wells. Smiling. God, that was the best thing ever. Maybe not the best. The best was him kissing me. Why did I have to go and ruin it? And what was I planning on discussing with him this morning, anyways? Was I going to ask if he still thought I was a "depressed social climber with no life"?

I turn the car on and drive down the tree-lined highway toward the academy. When I drive past the Whidbey Inn, I notice a police car in the parking lot. For a moment I think it's those detectives, Abbott and Baker. Maybe they've found the missing girl. My pulse quickens, and I slow down as I pass the motel. But it's not the pair of detectives. It's a young officer who has pulled someone over and is writing them a ticket. No one lost has been found.

I stop at the Whidbey Coffee Company, driving through the to-go window. I order a blueberry muffin and cappuccino, thinking carbs might curb my anxiety. I sit in my car, parked in the lot, and drink the coffee. I don't want to be inside the café. It's all sunshine and rainbows, the baristas overly peppy.

When my phone rings from my pocket I jump, but smile when I see it's Freddy.

"Where are you?" he asks.

"In Coupeville, getting coffee. You?"

"I'm headed there myself. There is a tarot card reader I want to meet."

"You? Tarot cards?" I suppress a snort that will do nothing but piss him off. "What are you talking about?"

"I think Wells knew this woman and I want to find out if she knows anything."

"About what?" I ask.

"About whatever the hell is going on."

"With what?"

"With what? God, Tippy, are you an idiot? With Wells and this missing girl. Things aren't adding up. And I'm freaking the hell out, to be perfectly frank with you."

I frown. Freddy is not usually a take-charge kind of guy. He is pretentious and witty and well-read. He is not a small-town detective for chrissakes.

"Who is with Wells?" I ask, refusing to comment on his hysterics.

"He doesn't need a babysitter."

I sigh, exasperated. "Not a babysitter, but perhaps a friend, some company, a cup of tea?"

"I don't want to fight. I know this is stressful," Freddy says. "I know you want things to be back to normal with Wells, but, honestly, Tippy, we can't rewrite history to make this better."

"Do you have to be so dramatic?"

"Tippy, I am not being dramatic. I am focused on the facts. We can't make up our own version of last fall."

My defenses flare, and with reason. "It feels like you are saying I don't remember what happened."

"I don't think it's possible for either of us to forget. If only we were like Wells and didn't have to remember." His words are sharp. "You slept with me and told Wells it was a one-off."

"I never imagined it would get so bad," I admit, my voice going soft. "I never wanted to hurt either of you."

"Well, when he found out after he moved that it was more than that, he said he'd never forgive you. You kept going back and forth with him and bickering all summer, and most of the fall. Of course it would hurt him."

"I know I hurt him. It's why he cut me off. Basically blocked me."

"No, Tippy," Freddy says, exasperated. "He cut you off because of whatever was happening with his students!"

"Don't say that," I say, my words lost in my shaking voice, the idea of Wells wanting to hurt me so unfathomable, even now.

Tears run down my cheeks and I am so relieved I am not face to face with Freddy right now because I swear to God I would slap him. He always knows how to cut one inch too deep.

I shove the muffin in my mouth and start my car. Screw Freddy and his opinions. Forget that I have covered his back hundreds of times with our parents, made excuses and apologies.

I don't need Freddy if he is going to treat me like I am something that can be disposed of. I just need Wells.

CHAPTER 24. FREDDY

My whole body trembles. This is not like me. At all. I cannot believe I let Tippy have it like that. I can bet what she is doing right now. Writing me off forever, driving to the cottage and attempting to seduce Wells. Which is really disturbing considering our old friend doesn't even have his memories of just how much he can't stand her.

Maybe I should have clarified, told Wells the absolute truth. That he was royally pissed at both of us after hearing about our indiscretion. Or whatever you want to call sleeping with your stepsibling.

The thing is, it's not the familial ties that have me ashamed. I couldn't care less about norms imposed by society. I met her when I was a teenager for God's sake; she was never my sister in any real sense.

I am, however, ashamed that I let it go on for so long, that I even wanted it — her — in the first place. It's Tippy! Tippy with her berets and Parisian airs and novel she will never finish. Tippy who drives me crazy and makes me mad and full of fire. Like I just was on the phone. She gets a rise out of me like no one else on this planet, and maybe she is more like my sister than I would like to admit, which just makes me feel one thousand percent worse.

Fuck.

I park the car at Marjorie's Magik, a small residence with new-age signage out front. *TAROT. CRYSTALS. FULL MOON CIRCLES*. I walk up a stone path and knock on the front door. There is no indication of the business hours and I have never been to a tarot reader before to know what I ought to do at this precise moment.

"Come in," a warm voice calls. "Sorry, I was on the phone with a client." A woman opens the door, dressed in athleisure, her long dark hair in tight braids. Her eyelashes are obviously not her own, but they make her golden-brown irises even more captivating. She is not what I was expecting in any version of my imagining. I was picturing flowy robes, a turban and fingers covered in rings. She unwrites every stereotype in the best possible way.

"Are you Marjorie?"

"That I am," she says in a sing-song voice. "And you are?"

"Frederick Rooper," I say, cleaning my feet on the welcome mat, then entering her home as she waves me in.

"I never saw you around before. New to town?" She lifts an eyebrow.

"Not exactly, here visiting a friend. A friend I am hoping you may know."

She twists her lips. "Try me."

"Wells Halifax. He is a teacher at Glennmare. He—"

"How is he?" she asks, cutting me off. "Everyone is talking about how he was helicoptered to Seattle. Horrible to hear."

"He's home, thankfully, but he has amnesia. The doctors are hoping his memory returns in a few days."

"Oh my God, he must be a mess."

"He can remember everything except the last six months or so. Since he moved here." I run a hand through my hair, my fear at what Wells has done mounting. Bernie was so odd in our conversation at the stables. Insinuating things I don't want to imagine.

"I see." Marjorie looks at me more closely now. "Do you want to sit?"

"Sure." I kneel opposite her on a cushion on the floor.

"How did you know about me?" she asks.

"One of the girls at the academy mentioned visiting you."

"Yes, many of the girls there come to see me." She smiles across the ornate red-and-black coffee table that's between us, filled with incense, candles, wax drippings, a burgundy velvet runner. It is a complete juxtaposition to Marjorie herself, who looks like she is about to go for a jog.

She must notice me staring. "I'm a personal trainer on the side. Rise and grind, you know?"

Without further comment, she begins to shuffle a deck of tarot cards, then hands them to me. "Hold them a bit; they need your energy."

"My energy?"

She smiles. "You're a skeptic? So was Wells. That man was a firecracker, though. He wanted to know everything about the cards and once I started to explain them, how they work, the hero's journey, he was all over it. I bet he knows more than me now. His brain is like a sponge."

I nod, moving the cards in my hand as I listen. "He's a lifelong learner. Before coming here, to teach at Glennmare, he was going to work on his doctorate."

"Ooh la la. And you, Mr. Frederick? What do you do?"

"I'm in law school."

She smiles as she takes the cards. Her nails are neon green, pointy and encrusted with crystals. "And you hate it, right? Wish you could get on a sailboat or some shit and just go?"

I swallow. "How did you know that?"

She shrugs. "You're from the East Coast, rich as fuck with a Rolex, and I know your twenty-something ass didn't buy it with cash you earned. You're living off your daddy, who you probably hate, and you're sick of life because you haven't yet lived."

I press my lips together, taking this woman in. "You are very good at your job, Marjorie."

She laughs, full belly-laughs, then shakes her head. "Sir, I'm not working, I'm just reading the room. You are tense! I think you need to lighten up."

"You think?" I snort, moving to sit cross-legged, which I haven't done in twenty-odd years.

"And I think you need to add some yoga to your exercise routine. Your joints are pissed."

Feeling more relaxed than I have in a long time, I smile back at her. "I'll try to remember that."

"So you need a reading?"

I shake my head. "Actually, I was just wanting to know about Wells."

Ignoring me, she makes a plan. "How about we do a past, present, future three-card spread?"

"Is that what you gave Wells?"

She frowns. "You're really concerned about him, huh?"

"He's my best friend. He has no one else but my sister and me."

The look she gives me suggests she knows more than she's letting on. "I think he's got more than that. That man was in love."

"Love?" I swallow. "With who?"

She shakes her head. "Wouldn't say, but I could tell."

"I don't doubt it, considering how well you read me."

She flips one card over. "Past. It's the Eight of Swords."

"Quite grim." I look at the card. It's a man wrapped in bandages, blindfolded, with swords plunged in the puddles around him.

"It represents bondage, feeling isolated or trapped, limited in your past."

I swallow. My entire childhood has been summed up in one card. "That tracks."

"And the present," she says, flipping a second card. A smile spreads across her face. "Judgment."

I frown. "That sounds hostile."

The card depicts an angel trumpeting a horn to the open-armed people below.

"This card marks the beginning of an awakening," Marjorie explains. "A time when a season of your life comes to an absolute end, making way for new beginnings. It's a good card."

"I don't know how this works. Am I supposed to tell you if I agree?"

"You can do whatever you like."

"I suppose it's promising."

Marjorie nods. "More than a promise. It's a fresh start. And maybe that is what you need . . . the sailboat, riding off into the sunset."

I grin. "I'll take it. And the future?"

She flips over the final card, this one the Knight of Pentacles.

"Makes me think of Wells," I tell her.

"Why is that?" she asks, her tone lower. "What do you see?"

"A man on a horse, for one. That's Wells. He moved to my parents' home last year, while deciding if he wanted to pursue his PhD, so he could ride more. He is exceptional with animals."

"He's mentioned the stables at Glennmare. The students at the academy riding their horses is a usual sight on the island."

"It's not just the horse, it's the armor," I say looking at the card. "Wells has always protected himself, made sure he was safe. What does the pentacle mean in tarot? I would think it's a talisman?"

"In tarot, the pentacles represent money. But I suppose everyone could interpret things differently."

"Wells has never been concerned with money," I say.

"Why would he when he has friends in high places?"

"It's my name that makes you think that?"

Marjorie nods. "Rooper Inc. owns like half the internet, right?"

"Something like that."

"I got a bit obsessed with Bitcoin a few years ago."

I smile softly, looking at the past, present and future cards.

Marjorie runs her fingers over them. "You know, this was a reading for you. Not for Wells."

"Which means?"

"The Knight of Pentacles wasn't his card. It was yours."

I roll my neck, exhausted with not knowing who my friend really is or was. "I wish it was his. It would help me understand him."

"Maybe it's time for you to let go, Frederick. His problem isn't yours to solve."

"Perhaps you're right." I pull out my wallet and hand her a hundred-dollar bill. "Thank you, for everything."

She takes the money and slips it into a small box on the table. "I would see the girls from Glennmare, from time to time, you know. His students?"

"Oh?"

She nods, her face tight. "I know what it's like to be a teenager. And have one, even. My son is a sophomore at Oak Harbor High. Anyways, one of the girls, Katherine, came in once, alone. She didn't care so much about tarot as much as some old ancient rite. Stuff I don't know about. Later, I mentioned it to Wells and he got really sad, told me to be gentle with Katherine because she was so innocent, that she tended to get carried away. Something like that. I brushed it aside because, honestly, those girls are none of his business outside the classroom."

"You know Katherine Calloway has been missing since Friday night, don't you?"

Marjorie's glittering eyes now darken. "I don't keep track of the news, but my spirit guides have been warning me of something sinister."

"Do you know where she might be, might have gone?"

I can see her mind working, putting pieces in places neither of us wants them.

"Do you think . . ." She starts, then stops. "I mean, I know this is ridiculous but, I wondered about this before, and now . . . you know how I said Wells was in love with someone . . ."

"It's complicated. Wells had his accident the same time she disappeared. He can't be harboring her in some love shack; he doesn't even remember she exists."

"Sorry," she says, pressing her fingers to her temples. "That was totally out of bounds. I shouldn't have said anything."

"No," I assure her. "It's okay. And, honestly, I've been having the same kind of thoughts since I arrived."

CHAPTER 25. DETECTIVE LEONARD ABBOTT

The text from Cassidy is unexpected. *Can I go over to Justin's after school?*

I'm with Phoebe, at the police station. We've just been briefed on the Katherine Calloway situation and it's not looking good. The search parties haven't found any leads.

Yesterday, after interviewing the man who admitted to buying wine for Katherine last Friday afternoon, we let him go. While he bought a minor alcohol, we let him off with a warning since he had no priors and he was wanting to help us with the case.

He said he never went anywhere with her, that she came and went on foot and that he simply helped her out when she was at the gas station. He was worked up about it all, that's why he came forward, was scared something bad happened to the kid and it was his fault.

The man has no record of any kind, and he's local, so in case we have reason to doubt his statement he is easy to track down. Overall, the interview was a disappointment because it got us no closer to the only thing that matters — which is finding Katherine.

I reread the text from my daughter and sigh. Really, we're dealing with boys now?

"What is it? News on Katherine?" Phoebe asks.

I show her my phone screen. She smirks. "So what are you gonna tell her?"

I begin to type, then press send. *Thanks for asking. Do you need a ride home?*

"Are you trying to be dad of the year or what?" Phoebe teases me as she reads the text I sent.

"What, you think I'm being too nice? I can be a hard ass, if that's what you're saying."

She shakes her head. "No. Play it cool, but run a background check."

"Justin lives down the street. Known him for a decade."

"Kids change, just make sure he's cool."

I nod, accepting the advice even if I don't want to imagine my little girl changing. "Any update from the clinics?"

"There was nothing. Every Planned Parenthood, every ER, every office in a hundred-mile radius has been called."

I shake my head, hating this part of my job. "Maybe we bring the roommates in for another interrogation?"

"We can do that. I'm wondering if the pregnancy angle was their way of sending us on a wild goose chase, though. Because it worked. We've been contacting clinics for twelve hours."

"That girl, Diane, she's a good actress if this is all bullshit."

Phoebe rubs her eyes. "Can we get coffee before we go to Glennmare?"

"Yeah, okay, I'll drive." Once we're in the car, we focus on the day ahead. We pull through Whidbey Coffee Company before making our way through the farmlands of the island, toward the property.

"Playing devil's advocate, why lie about something with such big implications?" Phoebe asks. "It's one thing to lie about who you're hanging out with after school, but to make up a story about your best friend getting an abortion? That isn't normal."

"So you believe the pregnancy story?"

"At this point we have literally no other leads." She shakes her head, frustrated. "There's nothing to go on."

"So we talk to the cook again," I suggest.

"You know her daughter that died?" Phoebe asks. "I looked her up — she's from Idaho like she said. Her teenage daughter died by suicide three years ago. She moved here shortly after, for this job."

"You don't think she was somehow involved in Katherine's disappearance?" I ask. "Because I honestly didn't get that from her. She just seemed like a busybody, but she does seem like she always needs to be in control."

"I don't think she has Katherine locked up somewhere, no, but I think she may know more about these girls than we realize. And like you said, we have no other leads."

When we get to the entrance, a group of students are sitting on the big front steps. They watch us, silently, as we enter their school.

"That's eerie," Phoebe whispers, leaning close.

"Very." Inside, Glennmare has a very different atmosphere than it did this weekend. Now, with classes in session, students are hurrying about, carrying huge stacks of books. It's eleven in the morning and it appears the students are just finishing up one lesson and heading to the next.

"Good day, I hope," Headmaster Duncan says, reaching to shake our hands when we come upon him in the hall. "Any news on Katherine?"

"We're working on it, sir. Can you help us locate Johanna, the cook? We have a few questions for her."

"For Johanna? Whatever about?"

"It appears she hears a lot of the goings-on here," Phoebe says. "Have you noticed that?"

Duncan runs a hand over his long, thick beard. "Yes, I suppose I have. She is quite the observer — and she can make a mean shepherd's pie."

"Good to know. Can you direct us to the kitchen?" I ask, wanting to cut to the chase. While we've interviewed Johanna in the kitchen before, I want to take the opportunity to walk through the halls with the headmaster, in case we can glean anything from him. At this point, I am desperate for any sort of clue.

"Of course, you must have a busy day ahead of you. And please," he says, indicating the corridor that leads to the kitchen, "if I can be of any assistance, don't hesitate to reach out."

Once we arrive, Duncan takes his leave and we turn toward the cook. "Johanna," Phoebe says. "We need to have a few words with you."

Johanna wipes her hands on her apron. "Now's not a good time. I have the biscuits to bake."

I look around — there is no dough sitting on the counter, the kitchen looks clean and tidy. I sense she just wants us gone.

"Would you prefer to chat at the station?" I ask. "Because that's the alternative."

"I'm not making coffee this time," she says with a furrowed brow. "I told you plenty and yet somehow it wasn't enough."

"Katherine has been missing for sixty hours. If you know anything about what she might be doing, now is the time to speak."

Johanna sits, and we join her at the table. Her eyes are rimmed in red, like she's been losing sleep, and her hands shake. She laces her fingers to still them. "Kitty trusted me."

"That makes sense," Phoebe says, pacifying the woman. "You're probably like a mother to many of the students here, so far from home."

Johanna's shoulders straighten just a touch with that comment and I look at Phoebe appreciatively. She sees things I don't, catches angles I would miss.

"The thing is," Phoebe continues. "A good mother would always make sure their child was safe. And the fact is, Katherine has been gone a long time. She's eighteen, which makes our job more difficult. She's an adult and she may not want to be found . . . but what if she does? What if she is in a bad situation right now and needs help?"

I expect Johanna to lash out at that, but she doesn't. "Maybe we do need some coffee after all." She stands and begins to make a French press, then she slices apple pie and brings it to us on plates. "The thing is," she begins. "You're right, I do think of these girls as my own. They have no motherly guidance. Even the night monitors are just a rotation of the female staff."

Originally we thought talking to the staff who watch the halls at night would be helpful, but they've given us nothing to work with. They say the academy is quiet after nine, that no one leaves their rooms, but, considering these girls are teenagers, they can't be paying very close attention to what's really going on.

We've gotten statements from them about Katherine's behavior, but no one had anything of note to say. She was a teenager, a rebellious one at that. Yes, they knew she drank from time to time, she was outgoing and a bit feisty, and she seemed to be the leader of the friend group, but not in a way that raised any red flags.

She never ran away, let alone burned bridges with any of the staff. Yes, she was a handful, but many of the girls here were.

When we shared the gas station footage with them, they weren't exactly shocked. Surprised at Katherine's actions but chalking it up to teens being teens.

The truth is, most people are so lost in their own little worlds they aren't really looking too hard at anyone else's. And many people who move, to an isolated island, are leaving something behind. The last thing they are going to do is look for trouble if they are here to forget the past.

Johanna brings over the coffee, along with a pot of thick pouring cream for the pie. "So, where were we?" she asks. "Oh yes, the trouble Kitty is in."

"So you know she is in trouble?"

Johanna peers into her coffee cup. "I hate to tell you this, but it's the honest truth. I didn't mention it before because I wanted to protect Kitty. She confided in me, and

I wanted her to feel safe to share, but I think you're right. I don't want her to be in harm's way."

I want to tell her to get on with it, but I also want her to keep talking. "So what did she confide, exactly?"

"Last week she came to me in tears. It was so heartbreaking to see her so distraught, but she could trust me, you see, knew I was someone she could rely on." She presses a hand to her chest. "She'd gotten herself in a bit of trouble."

"What sort of trouble?" Phoebe asks, taking copious notes of everything Johanna says.

"She was with child, poor doll."

Phoebe and I both sit back in our chairs; I take a sharp breath. We knew this already, from Diane, but to hear another person confirm it surprises me.

"Do you know who the father is?" Phoebe asks.

"I didn't ask and she didn't say," Johanna says, lifting a bite of pie to her lips. "Listen, I do not want it to get around that I shared this highly confidential information with you. The girls need to know they can confide in me, but, well, she should have returned by now."

"Do you know when she left?" I ask. "Or where she was going?"

"The girls mentioned that she was leaving Saturday morning, of course she must have left earlier, Friday night, at some point, I suppose, because no one has seen her since."

"They told you this directly?"

Johanna purses her lips. "Well, not in so many words, but I gathered it from what I overheard. They had plans that night."

"And where was Katherine going?"

"She needed a procedure," Johanna says delicately. "To take care of the pregnancy."

"And did you inform the headmaster of this? The nurse on staff? Surely there is protocol in place to keep students safe." I think of my daughter and her school. The adults there are mandated reporters and work to safeguard the students. I understand Glennmare operates differently than a public institution, but this is downright negligence.

107

Johanna's cheeks redden. "I'm not a teacher or a doctor. I'm not required to report anything, if that's what you're asking. I'm a cook, that's all. She needed help, so I gave it to her."

I pounce on that. "First of all, Katherine is eighteen so there was nothing to report. But how did you help her, exactly?"

"Well, I . . . I." Johanna shakes her head, looking caught in a web I can't quite trace. "I gave her money for the procedure. I did what any mother would do."

Phoebe's nostrils flare. "A mother would not send a child off in the night to get an abortion alone. I'm no parent, but that is *not* what a mother would do."

I have never seen Phoebe like this. She has passion, fire, sure — but fury is not an emotion I have seen in her in the two years we've worked together.

"Baker, do you need a moment outside?" I ask.

She shakes her head. "No, I'm good. But I'm done here. Johanna, if we need to speak with you again, it will be at the station. Understood?"

Phoebe pushes away from the table and walks straight out the back door of the kitchen. I gather her notebook and her pen and follow suit.

Outside, on the cold, dead grass, we stand, eye to eye.

"What was that?" I ask her.

"That woman is bad news, Leonard. Anyone trying so hard to get teenage girls to like them is dangerous. I don't trust her at all."

"You think she's involved in what happened to Kitty?"

Phoebe shakes her head. "No. She's got her head too far up her ass for that."

CHAPTER 26. DIANE

We sit in our room during lunch break, our hearts wrecked.
The candy stash under Coretta's bed is diminishing because
eating sweets is the only thing helping as reality sets in. Kitty
is not here. She is gone. But where? We are all falling apart,
one after the other. I broke first, like a fool, in front of the
detectives. But this is all going too far. I keep thinking I can
make myself unsee things . . . but it's impossible. When I
close my eyes, I see ruin. Everywhere.

Being melodramatic won't help things. We are realists,
mostly. It's Kitty who has the flair for drama. Me? I feel like
I messed everything up. The detectives are back, we saw them
pull onto the property and now we are just waiting for the
other shoe to drop. Guilt gnaws at me because I am the one
who broke our promise to keep everything a secret — to take
it to the grave.

"Let's go speak with Marjorie," Jolie suggests. "Maybe
she knows where Kitty is."

"She's not a psychic. She's a tarot reader, and not even
a good one," Bernie replies.

"So you suggest we do nothing?" I ask. "We just wait?"

Just then Coretta enters the room, her eyes wide. "Well,
you can stop feeling bad, Diane. I was just eavesdropping

outside the kitchen. Johanna told the detectives Kitty was pregnant and that she gave her money."

I fall into my bed, my head on my fluffy down pillow, feeling more scared than ever. Tears fill my eyes. Kitty has to come back. She has to.

"We didn't start this," Jolie says. "We can't feel bad."

Bernie frowns. "We let her go. That was our mistake."

"You think she's in serious trouble?" Coretta asks. "Because the detectives have no leads. If she's truly in danger, who's going to find her?"

"We have no money, no friends outside of the school, we can't exactly go on a crusade looking for her in the streets of Seattle," Jolie says.

"We could call our parents, explain what's going on?" Coretta suggests.

I roll over, looking out the window. The Salish Sea in the distance. I press my palm to the windowpane. Icy cold.

"What would you tell your parents, exactly?" Bernie says. "Because I'm stuck on that. They will ask questions. Like how did Kitty get pregnant at an all-girls school? Next thing you know, we'll all be shipped off somewhere else." She begins to cry. "I don't want to lose you, this. I love this place."

I want to comfort her, but I don't have the energy. I'm exhausted. The last few days have stolen all my emotional reserves. Have wrecked the way I see myself. I thought I had a moral compass — but then I let this happen. I could have done something. Instead, I stood silent.

"Kitty's parents are going to find out any minute now that Johanna corroborated Diane's story," Coretta says.

"Can they legally do that?" Jolie asks.

"I think the cops can do whatever they want," Bernie says.

"We should never have let Kitty talk us into going to the cabin Friday night." Coretta's face falls as she says the truth out loud. "We knew it was a bad idea, but she was . . ." She loses her steam. Lost in the memory of what happened Friday night.

We sit then, in silence. Remembering. The smell of death, for one, is seared into my nostrils. Am I going to live with this scent forever in my mind? I wish we could rewrite everything. Start from the beginning.

"If we call our parents, they are going to make us leave. We all know that. So we need another solution," Jolie says, lighting a joint.

"Getting high is going to help with the brainstorm?" Bernie says, her brows furrowed.

"It will help my creative thinking," Jolie says, walking over to Bernie and wrapping an arm around her. "Breathe in, baby, it will help you relax, too."

"I don't want to relax." Bernie is crying now. "I want Kitty."

I begin to cry then, too, softly, into my pillow. Coretta runs a hand over my hair. "It's okay, love, she will come back. You know Kitty, she was unpredictable."

"Remember last year, when she became obsessed with us buying vintage prom dresses for the end-of-year formal?" Coretta asks. "I forgot to buy one and she called my cousin, Tallie, telling her how I was the one who had ratted her out to our parents?"

"Oh, when Tallie was stealing your mom's oxy?" Bernie says, remembering.

"Yeah, and after that I swore I would never give Kitty my secrets again. She is too . . ."

"Controlling?" I ask, feeling like I am betraying my friend by even saying such a thing. But she is controlling. The morning I didn't want to let her use my notes for our geometry final — because I wanted to use them — she snuck a laxative in my yogurt. She smirked when I had to rush out of class for the bathroom. Later she told me what she did.

I was confused about why she'd tell me.

"Because people who love one another hold each other accountable," she said.

I didn't like how this conversation made me feel, but I didn't know how to stop it. "You could have taken notes yourself, Kitty."

She shook her head, her shiny hair swishing at me. God, she was always so beautiful. "Diane, it was all a test. I had the notes. I just wanted to see if you were loyal."

"So now you think I'm not?" I asked, aghast. My friends were my world, my identity. I didn't want to lose this, them.

She smoothed my hair down, looking adoringly into my eyes. "No, darling, now I think you understand what it means to be my friend."

"I do," I whispered back, taking her hand in mine. "I will never let you down again."

Now Kitty isn't here, and I know I let her down. We all did. That is why I don't think she will ever come back.

"She was unpredictable, sure. But she was also bipolar," Jolie says, her lips turned down.

Bernie squirms. "She may have been unpredictable, but she was on some sort of medication."

"Can you be certain she was taking it?" Jolie asks. "And don't you think Glennmare should have organized a therapist for her? I mean, her parents thought all this farmland and the salty ocean and the horseback rides were going to keep her healthy, and they were to an extent, but she should have been checking in with a doctor or something, right?"

"We don't know everything Kitty got up to," Coretta says. "She may have been meeting with a therapist and just didn't want to tell us. She didn't want us to know she was on meds, remember?"

"If she didn't take her medication, and she's been gone this long . . . she might be in a really bad place, mentally," Bernie says.

If I had the strength to talk, I would tell her I agree. Kitty is in trouble, and we have no way to help her. When the police came and searched Kitty's room, they said they didn't find anything — but would they have told us if they did?

Last summer, when we all returned to campus, we realized Kitty was dealing with mental illness. She was having a hard time, her parents were going on a trip to Belize with her younger brothers, and she wasn't invited. She said she didn't care, but we knew she did. She broke down, crying, saying her parents thought she was crazy and that if lobotomies were still a thing, her dad would probably shove an ice pick in her skull himself.

She was sobbing, and I wrapped her in my arms and ran my hand over her hair. The girls all gathered in my bed, on my white lace duvet, and we sat, holding our dearest Kitty.

From my experience, when people are falling apart, you need to hold them, and listen. If they fall to the floor, they will find it near impossible to stand once more. My mom is a drunk, and all my life I tried to pick her up. Eventually, though, I began to be the person she blamed for everything she hated in life, and my hands were no longer the ones she wanted to hold.

I made a promise to myself, when I met the girls here, that I would be stronger than I was with my mother. Even if it got difficult to be their friend, I would be constant, steady. I would hold on tight. I wouldn't let go.

Then I went and broke in front of the detectives, telling them about Kitty's pregnancy.

I am so damn weak and I hate it and I just want to be strong. Stronger than my mom.

Kitty loved Wells and we loved Kitty and we were unable to tell her no.

Except Wells. He told her no.

And that was the last time we saw him with his memories.

CHAPTER 27. WELLS

Alone in the cottage, I decide to look for the letters from Freddy. The ones the girls say he sent last fall. I've just opened my desk drawer when Tippy comes in. She's clearly upset about something; her eyes are red. She walks right to me and wraps her arms around my neck. Crying against me, she tells me she is sorry. For everything.

"Sorry for what, exactly?" I ask tentatively, pulling away. "I know I'm missing pieces of the story, Tippy, but what ones?"

"You remember everything this summer, right?" she asks, holding my hand. It is a familiar hold, and I squeeze her hand back. We sit on my bed, Tippy taking off her overcoat, removing her scarf. She's wearing a white button-down shirt but her bra is black, and I can see her nipples, hard.

"Yes," I say, blinking away thoughts of the girl from my dreams. Katherine. I focus on Tippy. Here. Real. "I remember this summer. It's pretty simple, isn't it? We'd been sleeping together. I wanted to be a couple. You refused and went and slept with Freddy to get back at me."

Tippy's eyes darken. "And then you went and slept with Iris again."

"Does it matter who I slept with when you didn't want me?" I ask.

114

Tippy shakes her head, frustrated. "I wasn't ready then, Wells, to commit. I am now. I'm different."

Tippy and I had been sleeping together for months, and I thought it was all building to more — to a true love — which is all I had really wanted. I wanted to be loved unconditionally, maddeningly; I wanted to be needed the way I needed her.

She wanted me for sex — that was it. And God, that destroyed me. I wanted her love. Her devotion. She wanted to have fun. When she said we could never be more than lovers, I thought I would die. I was willing to risk everything for her, and she didn't even want her brother to know we were fucking.

"I don't know what happened last fall. Tell me." I only have Freddy's version. Now I want hers.

Tippy sits up straighter. "Why do you think you had a falling out with Freddy?"

I clench my jaw, run a hand through my hair. "Okay, so, some of my seminar students stopped by. They mentioned how I'd been upset with Freddy."

"You're going to trust a group of teenage girls?" She rolls her eyes. "Did you ask Freddy if there was a fight?"

"As a matter of fact, yes. He said that we wrote letters about it, and that was actually what I was doing when you came home, just now. Looking for evidence — because I am in the dark here, Tippy. And I hate it."

She sighs, reaching out to smooth my messy hair. "It doesn't matter now. You and Freddy were mad, but now it's water under the bridge."

"But do you know why? Why were we fighting?" I keep pressing, forcing her to admit it.

She swallows. I know her well enough to know that she does indeed have more to share. "After you left for Glennmare, I felt lost. So alone. And so Freddy and I . . . we . . . Look, he's my stepbrother. I'm not proud of it."

"You carried on sleeping with him?" My body tightens, realizing Freddy told me the truth. Part of me feels nothing.

Another part feels enormous jealousy. At both of them. I love them both, dearly, and to think of them being together, intimately, without me . . . it helps me understand how upset Freddy must have been when he learned I was sleeping with Tippy without him knowing.

The level of deceit involved in keeping my affair with Tippy secret was impossible to sustain. I realize now it's impossible to hide anything from friends. Eventually, the cracks become craters, and everyone falls in.

"Don't be mad, but, yes, we kept returning to one another. Without you, we both felt lost. I love him as a friend, as a brother, but nothing more. I didn't. I just . . ."

"So you were using him? You know he adores you. Dammit, Tippy. What were you thinking?"

"I *wasn't* thinking. Just like this summer, I wasn't thinking. Now I've had time to really think about things, and the truth is I do want to be with you, Wells. Truly."

I drop my head in my hands. The three of us have become so entwined, our hearts joined in ways that won't work.

"Maybe we can start over, Wells. Try again?"

"While Freddy is still in love with you?" I shake my head. "Tippy, it's impossible. It's over. Even without my memories intact, I know this for certain: pairing off will destroy us. Isn't that exactly why Freddy and I had a falling out? I thought you had chosen him."

Tippy pulls my hands to hers, forcing me to look into her blue eyes. "But don't you see, Freddy chose me over you. He still would. Every time. So why do you owe him anything?"

My body stirs, with need and memories — Tippy in my arms in her Paris apartment, making love in candlelight, the Eiffel Tower in the distance. The week in Madrid, the summer heatwave forcing us to take off our clothes for days at a time, icy showers together in the hope of cooling off. Our trips to their family's country house, when Freddy was out with his father, our bodies entwined, her mouth on my skin, her heart beating hard against mine. I wanted it to last forever. But nothing good ever truly lasts.

"There is a student missing, Tippy. A student I knew to some degree, and I feel like until my mind is clear — until I can remember — I can't make choices about my future. I am trying to simply get through the present."

"I love you, Wells." Tears fill her eyes, roll down her porcelain cheeks.

"I love you too, Tippy. And for now, that must be enough."

She nods as I wipe her tears away with the back of my thumb. She smiles through her sorrow. "It's plenty."

CHAPTER 28. DETECTIVE LEONARD ABBOTT

We decide to go for a walk. Clear our heads. We need it after the shitshow in the kitchen. We head to the waterfront, sitting down on driftwood. The sky is heavy and gray, it's freezing as fuck out here, and I know we are missing a piece to this puzzle. Nothing is adding up.

"This isn't going well," Phoebe says, stating the obvious.

Never in my career have I felt so defeated. Partly because there is never much trouble here, on this island, and partly because being a father of a teenage girl myself, I suddenly feel like I've failed.

"At least now we know how she had cash to leave," Phoebe says.

I run a hand over my stubble, thinking about everyone we've interviewed. "What school did the headmaster say his grandson played for? In Port Townsend?"

"I don't think he did." She pushes out her lips. "You think he could be hiding something?"

"Someone is. Did anyone actually check out this man's alibi?"

Phoebe stands, dusts off her butt. "Get up, old fart, we got work to do."

We walk back to the academy and, this time, instead of looking for Johanna in her warm kitchen, we head straight to Duncan's office. He is sitting behind a large oak desk, bookshelves surrounding him, with a large window that showcases the massive madrona trees on the property.

"Oh, do come in," he says.

"We have a few more questions. Would you rather speak here or at the station?" I ask him.

"Here is fine, please, take a seat. Do you need anything? Coffee, tea? Would you like to speak with another teacher or student?"

He is incredibly helpful and willing. Not the sort of behavior of a person hiding something. Still, someone is.

"The questions we have are for you, actually," Phoebe says as she takes out her notepad. "You mentioned being at a grandson's basketball game. What school does he play for and where was the game on Friday held?"

Duncan sits up straighter; he presses his hands together in front of him, fingertips touching. "He attends Port Townsend High School. It was a home game that night."

"Great, and who did you attend the game with? Family, friends?"

He swallows, less confident than he was moments ago. "My daughter. Do you need her number? Because I can write it down for you if you like."

"What's her name?" Phoebe asks.

"It's Lisa Admiral now."

"Of course. If you could jot down her number, that would be great."

Duncan takes a business card from his desk and writes a phone number on the back. "She is in real estate and works unusual hours."

"On another note, before we go, have there been incidents or reports of Katherine Calloway being involved in compromising behavior with any adults on staff?" I ask.

Duncan clears his throat. "Pardon me?"

"We want to know if there have been any reports of an affair between your missing student and a member of the faculty," Phoebe says more plainly.

"My God, what are you suggesting?" Duncan's cheeks go pink as he shakes his head. "Katherine wasn't like that . . . we would never condone that sort of behavior."

"We would never suggest that it's something you would condone," I say. "But have there been situations that—"

"Look, there were reasons Katherine's parents brought her here. Glennmare is a respite from the world, a sanctuary, as I am sure you have noticed these last few days. But her disorder does not mean she is sexually involved with a staff member!"

"Disorder?" Phoebe glances at me. Maybe this is the puzzle piece we've been missing.

I take a deep breath. "Her parents never mentioned a disorder, and certainly you have not until now. Do you understand how vital it is to gain a clear picture of the situation so we can locate this student quickly?"

"I do, I do, and I didn't realize her parents kept that information to themselves. They are private people who appear to have a difficulty with letting people in. Including their daughter." Duncan waves his hands in the air, in defense. "I'm not the parent, of course, I just know mental illness is nothing to be ashamed of. I pride myself on running a school with plenty of resources for students who are struggling."

"What was she struggling with? Exactly?" Phoebe asks.

"She was diagnosed bipolar. Which is a tricky diagnosis for adolescents. However, her parents were very uncomfortable with this label and they believed she would be better suited here than . . ."

"Than home?" I scoff, disgusted. Who are these parents, and do they have any idea what sort of damage they are doing by sending their teenager away because of her brain chemistry?

"When you say you have plenty of resources, can you walk us through them?" Phoebe asks pointedly. "Because if there is a therapist we can speak with, or a guidance counselor, we need to interview them. This really should have been made clear to us when the investigation began. We have spoken with the teachers we know she had classes with, and even the night monitors. All of that was done Saturday morning, directly after the missing persons report was filed by the night monitor. I'm frankly shocked at your lack of concern."

Duncan stands, begins to pace the room. "We had a counselor, but she left last summer and we haven't rehired the position."

"You didn't feel it was a vital staff member at a girls' high school?" Phoebe asks, unfazed with Duncan's obvious discomfort. This is why she is great at her job. She doesn't back down.

"The resources we offer are not distinctly professional ones. They are more therapeutic in nature."

"Fresh air and wholesome food?"

Duncan nods. "Exactly. We have a steam room, a cold plunge pool. We focus on the spirit — omitting technology and expanding minds."

"Was she medicated?" I ask.

Duncan nods. "Yes. There is a nurse who comes twice a day, from town, to administer medications to the students. We have no doctor on staff, however, and the prescriptions and updates to them are managed by the families and their private physicians. Glennmare is merely a reprieve from the rest of the world."

"And is there any way for the students to access more than a single dose of their medication?" Phoebe questions, pen poised to write down Duncan's answer.

"You would need to ask our nurse, Hannah Humphry, but, to my understanding, no. They are in a locked safe in the nurse's station."

"So, barring Hannah finding medication stolen, we can presume Katherine Calloway has been off her bipolar medication for three days?"

Duncan seems to suddenly realize the severity of the situation. "Dammit," he says, reaching for his phone. "I'm calling the nurse, right now."

CHAPTER 29. THE GIRLS

We can't just sit here, waiting, wishing. It's time.

After our lunch break, we tell our teachers we're unwell, and they look at us with pity. "We understand," they say. "Take care."

It's not a lie. We are unwell. Diane is the worst of us. We are all, in our own ways, overcome with uncertainty.

Is it our burden to follow our friend unwaveringly? Is there such a thing as too much? Too much passion? Desire?

"How should we phrase it?" Coretta asks. She is poised with pen and paper, but we are getting nowhere with the note. Her hair is tied back with a black ribbon, same as the rest of us. She wears a long skirt with a blouse tucked in, a wool vest tight to her chest.

Our clothing is distinct. It was Kitty's idea. Last year, after we all became friends, we were bored here at school. Then, on a lark, on a trip to town, we saw an old theater having a yard sale. Since we had some spare cash tucked in our pockets, we stopped and looked. Kitty was enamored with the costumes they were selling. She insisted we all buy some dresses from old productions, and our style was born.

We went home for school breaks looting vintage stores and second-hand shops online for anything conjuring a time that matched our technology-free education. When people read instead of scrolled, wrote instead of texted.

Why was Kitty so charmed with the period clothes? Was it an attempt to prolong her childhood? Maybe. And is that so bad? To want something you never had? Because none of us here had childhoods you'd write about with any sentimentality. They were callous and cold and a waste, really. There was no playing in rain puddles or making mud pies. That's why we love Glennmare so much. Deep down we are all craving something softer, something gentle. Something ours.

Wells said that's what we needed. It's why we packed picnics and took walks and met in the cabin with candlelight on the full moon. It's why he learned tarot to indulge our fantasies and why he plucked blackberries in late September, feeding them to us, laughing, to make us feel adored.

How could one man do so much for our self-esteem?

The yuletide festivities felt like the promise of more good things only eight weeks ago and now it feels like it wasn't the beginning, it was just the start of it all unraveling. Kitty becoming desperate. Wells feeling like he went too far. The rest of us watching, not sure how to support the two of them. Wanting to protect them but knowing it wasn't going to end well.

We never could have predicted it would end like this, though.

Bernie shuffles the tarot cards, pulling one. "For inspiration," she says, "on how to tell Wells everything."

She flips over the Knight of Pentacles. We trace the figure on the card, a man on a horse.

"It's not a white mare," Jolie comments.

We tense, looking at her. Remembering.

"Don't!" Diane presses her hands to her ears. "I can't . . . I don't . . ." She begins to shake. She is more traumatized than we realized.

What does it say about us that we aren't equally shaken? Equally fragile? It should terrify us, the thought. Are we more numb to reality than we ever realized?

"It's a sign, though, isn't it?" Coretta asks. "We should be meeting Wells. It's the best way forward. We need an answer and no more playing nice. We need the truth."

"You think he's lying?" Bernie asks. "That he knows more than he is letting on? Because he didn't recognize us. When we entered his room, he looked at us as if for the first time."

"I'm not saying he is a liar, but he left the cabin that night with Kitty and now she is gone and he says he simply can't remember. I need more than that."

"If he can't remember, maybe we jog his memory," Diane says, coming out of her malaise. "Maybe we show him what he did and . . ."

"Are you suggesting we reenact Friday night?" Jolie barks a sharp laugh. We've never fought like this and disagreed so often. It's painful.

But then the laughter stops and we turn toward one another, needing a plan.

Diane's eyes are hard, and it feels electric, the power in the room. "I'm saying he *has* to remember and so maybe it's time we make him."

CHAPTER 30. MARJORIE

I pull out the hundred-dollar bill from my money box. I'm going to use it to buy Justin new kicks. He's been secretly wanting a new pair, though he would never, ever ask. I saw him looking at some on his phone last night during dinner. I place the money in my wallet and stand, needing to shake my thoughts from the conversation I had earlier today with Frederick. Meeting my client for her personal training session should help.

Grabbing my keys, phone and wallet, I head to my Prius. The drive to her house is short. I've known Hannah for years, but she just hired me on January 1st. Everyone is gung-ho this time of year to work on their diet and exercise, and I appreciate the season of resolutions because it means things aren't so tight financially for Justin and me.

As I drive, Frederick is on my mind. He left my house an hour ago and I can't stop wondering if I should have said more. Even though I have nothing to go off besides my intuition.

The missing girl complicates my feelings. So does Wells Halifax and his memory.

Maybe it's for the best. Him forgetting. Maybe it's the Universe's way of offering him a rest. Not that I think he deserves one. Or doesn't. Maybe we all do really deserve a one-time-only opportunity to forget it all and start over.

Who would I be if I forgot?

I pull into Hannah's driveway, knowing the answer. Free.

Free from the niggling doubt in the back of my mind that I am not enough, because then I wouldn't have a long list of things I never did that I once set out to do. Didn't cut off Dad when I should have. Didn't finish my dental hygienist classes. Didn't choose a good father for Justin.

"Hey," Hannah says, opening her front door. "Louisa just went down for her nap so good timing. We've got an hour. It's been a weird morning."

Hannah is a nurse at Glennmare, but only two hours a day. She is paid well, she says, for such little work, and she is able to stay home with her toddler while her partner, Sam, works evenings.

I open my trunk and grab the yoga mats and the bag with hand weights. A few minutes later we are moving through simple stretches on her living room floor.

"So how come the morning was weird?" I ask.

"You hear about the missing girl at Glennmare?"

"Yeah, a bit."

Hannah moves in step with me, toe touches and moving into simple downward dogs to warm ourselves up. "The cops were just here, if you can believe it."

"Really?" My eyes widen. "Why?"

"I shouldn't say this, but you know I work there, right?"

I laugh. "Of course. It's a small island. Everyone knows everything."

"I bet you didn't know she was on lithium."

"Um, no, I did not. And I don't think it's legal for you to tell me."

Hannah grimaces. "I know. I suck, but it's all just so crazy."

Hannah and I begin a set of crunches, her face turned toward mine. "The girl's a sweetheart. I see her every morning, eight o'clock on the dot, and she's always smiling. Cheerful. She brings me flowers, like who does that? Or baskets of

126

berries. You know how that group of girls dress, like they are in an old-timey play or something? She would always be wearing cardigans and tweed dresses."

"Tweed? Sounds fancy," I say, taking this in. "And she's been gone since Friday? What do they think happened to her?"

"The cops didn't say, only wanted to know about her medical history, which I really have nothing on. I dole out meds, pretty simple."

"She's eighteen, right?" Hannah nods and I continue, "When I was eighteen, I had already moved out, was pregnant with Justin. Was an adult. Maybe she was done living like she was a character in a book from the 1800s."

Hannah laughs, then covers her mouth. "Shit, we can't wake up Louisa."

"I'm whispering, it's on you if she wakes, mama."

Hannah grins as we begin holding our planks.

"I feel bad for her, though," I add. "She doesn't come off like I was at that age. She sounds innocent."

"I'm not so sure she was," Hannah says. "I heard Bob Canyon admitted to buying her booze every week for the last year, down at Handy R's. That doesn't sound too innocent. And Bob told me he would see her with other guys too, men who were here for camping and hiking trips. But I guess he didn't tell the cops that because he didn't know anyone's names and didn't want to be wrapped up in it anymore."

"Huh." I frown. "That is sort of skirting the truth, though, isn't it?"

"Maybe, maybe not," Hannah says, tapping her fingertip to her chin, thinking. "If we don't have facts, it's just hearsay?"

I think about the moment I shared with Frederick earlier, when we both stood with the same thought in our minds . . . that there was a possibility Katherine was in love with her teacher, and vice versa. Neither of us spoke the entirety of the thought aloud, but I know he was on the same wavelength. "You think she was seeing anyone seriously?"

"Like, dating?" Hannah collapses on the mat. I release my plank, too. "Well, maybe she hooked up with guys when they came through town?"

"She came into my shop a few times. Wanting readings with her friends, but she came in alone too. I got the impression she was in love with someone. Her friends got pretty excited when I pulled the Lovers card for her once. They said it was a sign. An omen. Strange, right?"

"All the girls there are a little off. I mean, they are living in this very deprived state. They don't read the news or watch television. They get *obsessed* with topics because they literally have nothing else to do."

"I can't imagine Justin without his smartphone. He'd probably go insane from boredom."

There's a knot in my stomach at that thought. I never thought the girls were off. I thought they were looking for some fun when they visited me. But when Katherine came alone, it was different. Now the knot feels like a lead ball.

"What?" Hannah asks. "You look like you've seen a ghost."

"It's not a ghost, more like a premonition."

CHAPTER 31. FREDDY

The town is quaint, and I head to a pub that is open on the Main Street, overlooking the Sound. The conversation with Marjorie left me lost. Who is Wells? Really? And who am I to have been his faithful friend for so long?

Would he really have an affair with his high-school student? I take another swig of my Pilsner, not wanting to think of it.

Just as I've begun to eat my fish and chips, the pair of detectives who've been investigating this missing girl come in.

I offer a simple wave, not wanting to ignore them. Tippy may think I'm pompous, but I am not above being polite. Especially when these two officers are clearly doing what they can to figure out where the hell this poor girl is.

Detective Abbott walks toward me. "Frederick, right?"

"Yes. Abbott, Baker, nice to see you again."

They look me over quizzically, as if trying to place me. It might be that I'm slightly overdressed for a pub, the suit might be a bit much mid-day, but my options were limited.

"I got word a bit ago that my friend Wells has an appointment with neurology tomorrow in Seattle, so that's promising."

A waitress comes over, asking them if they'd like their usual Coke and hamburgers. "Sounds good," Baker says.

"Actually, a Caesar salad and water, please." Abbott shoots a look at Baker as if to say, *what?* "Trying to make some changes is all," he explains with a shrug. "The other day my co-pilot over here mentioned I had a beer belly, so." He smiles. "Mind if we sit?"

"Not all," I say, wondering if it is my ethical duty to say I am concerned about a possible relationship between my friend and a student. If there isn't one, what sort of person am I for questioning them? If there is, what sort of person would I be for turning a blind eye? "The view from here is fantastic." I nod at the big bay windows overlooking the cove, not knowing how else to proceed.

"Sure is. Say, you and Wells, how long have you been friends?" Abbott asks as the waitress delivers their drinks.

"About seven years. We met freshman year at Yale."

Abbott whistles. "Fancy. And now he is teaching out here at such an antiquated school?"

"He wanted a change."

"Why?" Baker asks.

I lean back, smiling. "Perhaps you'd like to ask him?"

They chuckle. "Sorry," Abbott says. "Just curious. And are you also a teacher?"

"No, I'm in law school. Though lately I've been wondering if I ought to get one of those boats, like the ones out there," I say, nodding to the water beyond the window, "and just . . . sail away."

"Running from something?" Baker asks.

I shake my head, unable to suppress a smile. This pair is good. They are both unassuming and absolutely spot on. They could go into business with Marjorie.

"Not running, more like, ready to begin again?"

"Would you do things differently?" she asks.

"Just bits. A chapter here and there. Not the overarching story."

"Are you a writer, as well as a lawyer?" Baker asks.

"No, that's my sister, Tippy. She's the aspiring novelist in the family."

Their food arrives and Baker speaks again. "I always wanted to write a book."

"Oh, yeah?" Abbott grins. "What would it be about? Small-town crime and the plucky young detective from the big city who solves the murder mystery?"

She tosses a French fry at him. "Hardly. I would write a historical romance set in Argentina. Sunsets, dancing in the street, an angry father, an arranged marriage. I don't know." She laughs.

Abbott, though, laughs right back. "Sounds like you do know, actually."

She rolls her eyes. "See what I have to put up with?"

"I was actually thinking how lucky you both are, to work together. To get along so well."

"Sounds like you have good friends too." Baker cuts her burger in two. "Wells and your sister."

"Yes, but you know how friendships go. Especially with friends from college. Over time, they change."

"True. I don't talk to my friends from the police academy so much," Abbott says. "When we were training, hell, I thought we'd all be thick as thieves for life."

Phones begin to buzz simultaneously and both detectives reach in their pockets. I watch as they read messages, presumably the same one.

"Is it about the girl?" I ask.

Abbott smirks. "No. It's about the headmaster."

I want to know more, of course, but they don't offer and I have no right to intrude. The waitress boxes up their food and they stand. "Enjoy the view for as long as you can," Baker says, her burger box in hand. "Soon enough the tide will change and it will never look like this again."

CHAPTER 32. JOHANNA

When I bring Duncan his afternoon tea and cookies, he is on the phone, practically spitting. "I don't care, Lisa. Deal with it." He slams his phone on his desk, glaring at me. "Did you say something? To the detectives?"

"About what?" I ask, backing out of the office, holding the silver tray and wishing I knocked.

"About me. About my work here." He is agitated, angry.

"No, I never mentioned you. Would you like me to? The detectives listen to me. They understand how vital I am to the running of Glennmare. They trust me. I can tell them—"

"No. Don't say anything. Not a word." His words feel like a reprimand, and I feel small for a moment, before remembering I know his secrets.

I step toward him, whispering, "Is this about the wire transfers?"

"I told you to shut up!" He presses his fingertips to his temples. "This is not your business. It never was."

"I've never told a soul and never would. You put your faith in me when you hired me and I put my faith in you."

Duncan Wright looks at me then as if he has never met me before. His face goes slack. "You're a cook, Johanna. Very replaceable. And maybe I should have done it already, because all you do is stalk around corners listening in. It's how you learned about my situation in the first place. You don't have boundaries."

My fingers wrap around the silver platter. It's thick and heavy and I could take one step forward and smash it against this man's head. I could walk away and clean the platter in my kitchen and no one would be the wiser.

Rage washes through me. How dare he say those things. *Replaceable?*

Duncan turns, looking out the window. I lift the platter. Ready to strike.

"Dammit," he cries. "The police are here. For me."

CHAPTER 33. DETECTIVE LEONARD ABBOTT

It took three hours from the time we checked into his alibi before his entire empire collapsed.

"He wasn't even good at it, embezzling money," Phoebe says as we watch officers enter Glennmare with a warrant for his arrest.

"Terrible, actually." I've been a part of enough arrests over the years to know it always causes a scene. However, I've never witnessed an arrest where nearly fifty teenage girls watched.

The scene, of all of them here, the wind picking up, the clouds parting, the winter sun shining down on their faces, it takes my breath away.

"What is it?" Phoebe asks.

"It's eerie, isn't it? All the girls out here, like this?" We're standing off to the side, away from the crowd. I scan the students, who huddle in groups around the grand entrance of Glennmare. The ones I am drawn to, though, are all dressed like they've turned back time. Long hair flowing, skirts billowing with the wind, eyes glassy.

"They look lost," she finally says.

"Don't all kids?" I ask, thinking of Cassidy. It's been a long few days. She's probably with Justin right now. Maybe

I should talk to his mom, make sure her son is on the straight and narrow if he's hanging out with my little girl.

"These ones look more lost than the rest."

"Guess money doesn't buy happiness, huh?" I say, watching as fellow police officers lead out Headmaster Duncan Wright in handcuffs.

"Damn. He looks like he aged a decade in a few hours." She bumps her shoulder with mine. "This is all thanks to you, you know?"

"I was hoping it would bring us closer to finding Katherine. I wasn't planning on opening up a massive embezzling scheme."

Once we confirmed his grandson wasn't on a basketball team, his daughter, Lisa, freaked out. When the cops arrived at her house in Port Townsend, she was shoving stacks of cash in duffel bags. Duncan had embezzled money from the school by adding new additional charges for food and guidance counseling — which were already included in the tuition fees. He needed the cash for his daughter's gambling problem and was willing to go to great lengths to help her. Only now, it had backfired.

The chief of police, Janice Richards, walks over to us.

"You think the school is going to shut down over this?" Phoebe asks her.

Chief Richards looks back at the school. "The board of the school has already sent an interim headmaster."

"Students staying put, then?" I ask.

"Far as I know," the chief says. "Though I'm guessing lots of these girls are going to be leaving over the next few days. A scandal like this, after the missing student? Doesn't put the school in a good light."

"Speaking of, is there any possibility of Katherine knowing about the headmaster's scheme?" Phoebe asks. "Is there a chance he could have been the one to get rid of her?"

"We are certainly going to interview him at the station to find out," I say.

"We will have him in a holding cell when you're ready for him," the chief says. "It's been a mess over there. A guy who was here camping last week is missing too."

135

I frown. "A kid?"

She shakes her head. "No. Late twenties. Sounds like a bit of a recluse from what the family says, but that he came here a lot to camp." Exhaling, she refocuses on the case at hand. "So nothing's come up from that teacher? It's a strange coincidence, right? Both things happening on the same night."

"It's proving difficult considering he has a form of amnesia," Phoebe says.

"Convenient."

"We think he may have been sleeping with Katherine," I tell the chief. She's already been briefed on the suspected pregnancy, but not on whom Katherine was sleeping with.

"And will anyone corroborate this theory?" Chief Richards asks.

My eyes scan the property, landing on the girls who share a room with Katherine. They are watching as the headmaster is led to a police cruiser. Their eyes are wide. They cling to one another, cold.

"Is this about Kitty?" one of them, Bernie, I think, calls out to the officer closest to her.

"No," he replies. "An entirely separate matter."

I watch as the girls' faces fall, as if hit hard by a truth they weren't expecting.

It would be easier, of course, if they knew where Katherine was, but that reaction tells me the hard truth of it.

No one knows where Katherine is, not even her closest friends.

CHAPTER 34. JOLIE

I knew the headmaster was good for nothing. Everyone did. That's why he was dubbed Dunky. And now he is literally ruining our entire lives because of his illegal schemes.

And no one is telling us anything. We are in the dark, standing outside Glennmare in broad daylight.

We never talk to anyone besides one another because we live in the middle of nowhere without phones. Besides, we're just girls. GIRLS! What do we know anyways except how to French-braid hair and draw heart eyes on our feelings?!

I hate this. All of it. Every single bit.

Where the hell are you, Kitty-Cat?

Last Friday it was exciting. At first. Kitty convinced us that Wells was willing, but, honestly, even if he wasn't, we told one another we would do it ourselves, without him. We could make ourselves the king! We didn't think she was serious. We wanted to play along. Not in a real sense, obviously. That would be psychotic, but we are young! In love! Deluded.

Now, none of that matters because she ran from the cabin sobbing and just flat-out disappeared. We went back to our rooms, covered in mud and memories, hating how far we let things go — how gruesome it became.

We looked through Kitty's things thinking there must be a clue. A sign. A tarot card balanced on the bathroom sink signaling her plan. But no. Nothing. She left everything behind. Her sticker collection and her pressed flowers and her favorite octopus stuffy named Pussy that always sits on the center of her bed. A nod to the childhood she never really had.

"I'm going to deliver the note," I tell the others.

"I'll come with you," Coretta says, and soon we're all going, which I don't mind, but, I did want to see Wells alone.

Not because I have a thing for him. God, no. I mean, I think he's the greatest man maybe ever, but he is (was?) Kitty's and besides, I don't exactly want a dick that close to me. What happened to Kitty? P-R-E-G-G-O. Also I'm a lesbian.

I wanted to see him alone because I wanted to corner him, hold a knife under his chin and demand answers.

Dramatic, maybe, but I am a girl, after all!

We look over our shoulders to make sure no one is following us. No one is. The other students at Glennmare are as demented as we are, but we love them all in their own way. There is no big bad bully here, nothing like that, because even though movies and stuff want everyone to think girls like to fight, it's really not true. We fight in real life (meaning NOT Glennmare, which is like an Amish paradise) because we are competing for attention from our parents, from boys, from teachers and bosses and doctors and maybe like everyone, actually.

But here we are not vying for anything. We can all do whatever the fuck we want and no one cares. I'm not saying I like Headmaster Duncan as a person — he was old-school in a grandfatherly way and it skeeved us out — but, like, he never bothered anyone. But it kind of makes sense if he's busted for embezzlement considering all the students have families that are loaded.

Here, we aren't trying to win anything. There is no prom queen or head cheerleader. Our math teacher reviews our tests and we have finals to submit, but we don't get, like, report cards with letter grades attached to them. Any stress we feel about our assignments is self-inflicted.

Here, we can do anything, and no one really cares. Sure, we have "night monitors", but the only reason they knew Kitty was missing was because we were freaking the fuck out and had to tell them.

And when I say we can do anything, I mean literally anything. We don't even try to get away with shit. No one really cares what we do. Kitty started getting us booze on the weekend because we decided we'd do a wine-and-cheese hour once a week where we all sat around smoking and drinking while writing our erotic novel that is seriously stupid but also kind of hot and all ours.

Yeah, we were drinking underage, but the night monitors knew, and Kitty loved the thrill of getting someone like Eli to buy her booze, and we indulged her even though we all said we'd take turns or even, like, ask Wells to buy the alcohol because surely he'd do anything Kitty asked, but she insisted this was her thing.

Kitty had lots of things, to be fair. Like an obsession with horse sacrifices, and other weird shit.

"The detective is watching us," Diane whispers as we walk behind the school toward the cottages. "Maybe Jolie should just go alone. It's too much attention."

"It's okay," I tell her, reaching for her hand, lacing her fingers with my own. "We're in this together, as it should be."

"And we should stay together, considering this might very well be our last night here," Coretta says.

"Don't say that," Bernie whines.

"It's the truth, though. They are gonna have to tell our families the headmaster just left the building in handcuffs. And the Kitty situation is terrifying. It's all only getting worse."

"Shhh. It's not over." I pull the piece of parchment from my pocket. "We have tonight."

CHAPTER 35. WELLS

The dream is much more erotic than the rest. The young women are surrounding me, all in white, touching me, all of me, in the cabin.

It's terrifyingly wonderful and I don't want to wake up, but I do when I hear a tapping on the window.

I sit up, my hand on my ribs, my head throbbing.

The young women from the dream are here for a second time. They push the window up.

"Are you alone?" the redhead asks. God, they are all so beautiful.

The thought alone makes me nauseated. Was I possibly immoral with these innocent girls?

I hold up a finger, very aware of my erection, and call out for Tippy. I stand, angling myself away from them, and listen for a reply. The shower runs.

"Tippy?" I rap on the bathroom door.

"Wells?" she calls. "I just jumped in — you all right, love?"

"Fine, I just woke up. Don't worry, I'll lie back down."

I walk back to my bedroom, closing the door behind me, locking it.

They don't crawl into my room this time and I'm glad. I was just in such a visceral dream state that I need to be more awake before they come closer. Am I still dreaming?

"I'm Jolie." The redhead smiles. "Take this."

"What is it?"

"Our plan is to help you get your memory back. We thought we could bring you back to the night where you lost it. We thought maybe it might help."

I take the paper from her. "Why do you care so much about helping me?"

Their faces collectively fall and I know I've said the wrong thing.

"For Kitty," the white-haired one says, tears in her eyes. "We need her back."

"Of course you do," I say, running a hand over her cheek, brushing her tears away. The impulsive gesture feels so familiar, it startles me. What is the nature of our relationship that I would so easily stroke her face?

She turns her head, ever so slightly, letting her lips brush over my palm.

"We miss you," she says. "We're scared."

"So am I," I whisper, stepping away from the window, from these ghosts, these visions, these girls from my dream who have me spellbound.

The shower water turns off. I swallow. "You have to go."

"We know." They slip away, without another word. They move beneath the rhododendron under my window, gone.

"Wells?" Tippy calls. "Did you need something?" she asks.

"I'm fine," I tell her, unlocking my door, taking her in. She stands wrapped in a towel, the woman from my past. I feel like a decade has passed since I held her against me, naked and mine. Now, I am a different man, no longer belonging to her.

I look over my shoulder, out the bedroom window. Feeling like I belong to someone else.

CHAPTER 36. DETECTIVE LEONARD ABBOTT

By the time I pull up to the house, I'm beat. The last few days have left me feeling like a failure. I can't find this girl and it's killing me. What if it was my daughter who was lost? I wouldn't want the cops giving up.

I bought this home the month after my girlfriend told me she was pregnant. Nothing fancy, but it's a good, solid house that could fit a family. A year after Cassidy was born, though, her mom split and we've barely seen her since. There were signs that she wasn't going to stick around to raise Cassidy, and I was surprised she even wanted to keep the baby — but, God, I'm glad she did. My daughter is the pride of my life.

When I get inside, I'm surprised to see Cassidy here on the couch with her homework spread out around her. At sixteen, she is the spitting image of my sister at this age. Thick, wavy blonde hair, eyes like a summer sky, a pair of dimples, beat-up Converse, overalls, a ringer T-shirt underneath. She could just as easily have been a teenager in the nineties.

"Thought you were hanging out with Justin?" I ask, sitting down in an armchair across from her.

"We got coffee downtown, but he could only hang out until four. His mom needed him to do some chores." Cassidy gets up, walks to the kitchen. "Want a Coke?"

"Diet Coke," I say.

She laughs. "Phoebe is giving you a complex, Dad." She brings me a can and a bag of pretzels.

"Justin and you pretty good friends?" It's hard not to imagine myself at Justin's age — going to the beach with friends and meeting the girls from Glennmare.

Cassidy closes her laptop, leaning back on the couch. "Yeah, we're kind of, like, together?"

I stiffen. Trying not to show my unease. "Together, like, a couple?"

She smiles. "Yeah, Dad, like a couple."

"I didn't know the two of you were close."

"We've been friends since we were five."

"And is he good to you?"

Her cheeks flare red. "I mean, he bought my mocha today?"

"That's nice. And look, I'm not trying to get in your business; it's just, you're my little girl, Cassidy."

"I'm sixteen. Soon I will be leaving, going to college."

I run a hand over my jaw. "Can we just stick to the present? I'm trying to wrap my mind around my daughter having a boyfriend. I don't want to think about you leaving the island."

Cassidy smiles. "Understood. But time flies, Dad. You need to prepare yourself for when you're an empty-nester."

"Woah." I chuckle. "Again — can we focus on today? How was school?"

Cassidy pulls out a paper from her binder. "Got an A minus on my chem test."

"Impressive."

She smiles. "Justin helped me study for it."

"I see, so you're telling me he's a good influence on you?"

"Yes, he is. He's never gotten in trouble or anything. His mom would kill him if he did anything stupid."

"Do you see his mom, Marjorie? Haven't talked to her in a long time."

"Not today, but sometimes? She's working like three jobs. The tarot reading thing, she does food delivery, oh, and she's a personal trainer." She grins. "Maybe you should hire her."

I laugh. "Funny."

"You know what Justin said? His mom gave tarot readings to that girl who went missing. The one you are looking for. Justin met her."

"Recently?"

Cassidy shrugs. "I don't know about that. Sounded like she and her friends liked to go get readings, though."

"Really, he wasn't just making up a story to impress you?"

Cassidy frowns. "Justin isn't a liar. It came up because everyone at school is talking about this girl."

"I don't think he's a liar, sorry, but it's my job to question things."

"Do you know where she went?" Cassidy asks.

"Katherine Calloway?" I shake my head. "No, but you've given me a lead, sweetheart." I set my Coke can on the coffee table. "Hate to ditch you, but I need to go talk to your boyfriend's mom."

Her eyes widen. "What, like, to make sure he's good enough for me?"

I smile. "No, I trust your judgment. I need to go talk to Marjorie to find out what the heck that girl was asking her."

CHAPTER 37. CORETTA

We take our time getting ready for our evening visit to the cabin with Wells. While I am just beginning to do my hair, our teacher, Ms. Ellis, comes to the door. "It's your turn, Coretta."

I set down my brush and look at the other girls. Bernie already spoke to her parents. Her eyes are still red from crying. Diane's too. Their parents said they have to leave tomorrow. It really is our last night together at Glennmare, except Kitty isn't here.

This entire year we have pretended we have suspended time. Like this will last forever — our seminar with Wells and watching love bloom before our eyes and Kitty sweeping us into her orbit. It's where I want to stay.

But now that Kitty is missing and our headmaster is gone and students are being sent home — it feels like the spell is finally broken. Whatever incantation Kitty put on us girls is starting to fade.

And the more I think about our friendship, without Kitty here to sway my emotions, I wonder if she was ever that good of a friend at all. It was always her way, and, with the fog lifted, I'm seeing more clearly. I want friendships that go both ways.

And even though our time here is getting cut short, soon enough we would all have been leaving anyway. School is going to end and we will be at different colleges, in different states — starting over. These petticoats and lace gloves will have no place at college. Which is fine — I can make peace with folding up capes and gowns and tucking them into a trunk — what I cannot lay to rest is my devotion to the other girls. They were just as much Kitty's pawns as I was.

Still, we have to find Kitty. Regardless of whether she was using us, she has no one else. What kind of girls are we if we stop caring in her time of need?

In the library, the faculty congregate on the far side of the room, drinking coffee and discussing the future. I smile at them as I reach for the phone in the center of a big oak table.

We usually do this on our assigned afternoon. We each get one phone call home a week, not because the academy is strict, but because they want our usage of electronics kept to a bare minimum. To better stimulate our young minds.

This is different, though. We are all calling our parents today. They've already received an email outlining the situation here, and the phone call is required to touch base.

"Dad?" I sigh. "It's me."

"Corey, hi. I read the email."

His inflection gives nothing away. But that isn't new; he is a man who's never given me much.

"Right, um, so what do you think?" I bite my bottom lip. "About the situation here?"

"Well, it seems like two separate situations. A headmaster who was embezzling money and a girl who has gone missing."

"It's my roommate," I tell him, my throat tightening. He has never asked a single thing about my life at Glennmare. It's hard to know how much to share with a man who doesn't know you.

"And have you spoken with the police? I presume there is an investigation underway?"

"A few times, yeah. I thought someone would have told you."

"The communication from Glennmare is spotty at best. I was surprised to receive this email from the school."

"What do you think I should do?" I feel small in ways I hate.

"You can stay there or come home. You're technically an adult, anyway. Caroline is due in three months, and the baby arriving will change the house, but you've been through that before."

My fingers curl the cord of the antique phone. My stepmother, Caroline, hates me at best.

"How's Mom? You think I could stay with her?"

My father exhales slowly. "You know that isn't an option. She is still in Barbados as far as I know, and you need to finish high school. You've already been early accepted to Wesleyan."

"You think I should stay put?" I ask, my heart sinking. It's not that I don't want to be here without everyone else. It's just, Diane came back from the call with her parents saying they were worried and didn't want anything bad to happen to her, and that they missed her so much anyway. Bernie's parents said this was the last straw. They already didn't like the fact they couldn't speak with their daughter any time they wanted to.

Diane and Bernie were both distraught, of course, that they have to leave, but also, I think, surprised to hear so much emotion from parents who for so long felt unreachable to them. In a state of worry, the number-one concern was their daughters' safety.

My father doesn't seem to care what happens to me one way or another.

"I think once again you are complicating things, Corey. It's always like this."

"I didn't complicate anything!" My voice raises, which is always the problem. I express myself, my father gets mad, I get punished. Trying to find an alternative, I suggest, "Maybe I could move to Grandma's for a while?"

He sighs. "She has enough on her plate with her health issues. It's not an option."

I bite my bottom lip, embarrassed that I didn't think about that. Grandma had hip replacement surgery a month ago and I haven't been good about checking in on her, I have been so self-focused.

"Look, Corey," he says. "I'm not sure what you want from me. My hands are tied."

"I want you to care one way or another that I'm okay. I'm a little scared, Dad. My best friend has been missing since Friday night. It's Monday!"

"Now you're getting hysterical. I can't deal with this. It's been a long day."

"I'm sure it has been up in your ivory tower."

He scoffs. "I wish you would grow up, Corey. You've had a silver spoon in your mouth all your life and still you make things difficult."

I wipe my stinging eyes. Why did I think this call would be any different?

"I'm sorry to make things difficult for you. You don't need to worry about me, though, okay? Like you said, I'm technically an adult. I can make decisions for myself."

"If you decide to come home, I'm told there is a liaison working on travel arrangements, but it seems best if you stay put, don't you agree?"

"Yes, Father."

I hang up the phone, looking over at the faculty. The woman who teaches both my French and government classes looks at me with sad eyes. I turn away. I don't need her pity. What I really wanted was my father to care what happened to me.

As I walk the long hallway, up the steps to the dormitories, I wonder if my dad didn't ask how I'm doing because he doesn't want to know the answer.

Maybe he already thinks of me as a lost cause.

But what would it be like to have a dad who thinks of you as *the cause*? Their reason, their pride, their joy?

I wipe my eyes again, not because I won't be leaving Glennmare tomorrow, but because, turns out, it's more than a school. It's the closest thing to a true home I've ever known.

CHAPTER 38. DETECTIVE LEONARD ABBOTT

I drive to Phoebe's condo to pick her up. The moment she opens the passenger door I begin to explain what Cassidy said.

"The girls have been holding tarot cards every time I see them," Phoebe says as she slides in and buckles up. "You notice that?"

I nod. "So, this tarot reader, Marjorie, I've known her for years. And I guess her son, Justin, is Cassidy's boyfriend."

Phoebe's eyes widen as she presses the button for the seat warmer. February on the island is frigid. "A boyfriend? Wow, this has been quite the day. Did she just tell you?"

"Yeah, when I got home."

"Did you play it cool?"

I chuckle. "I tried."

"I bet you did good. That girl is lucky to have you." Phoebe looks over at me and I appreciate her words. Sometimes as a single dad, I don't know if I'm being the person Cass needs. "Does she know we're coming?"

I shake my head. "Didn't even get that far. Was mostly focused on getting you and getting over there."

When we pull up at the weather-worn cottage where Marjorie has lived for as long as I've known her, I am looking deep down for a seed of hope. Right now, I feel like it's missing.

Knocking on her door, I look over at Phoebe. "Ever had a tarot reading?"

She looks at me like I'm crazy. "Of course I have. I'm a millennial."

I chuckle. "So am I, technically."

"If that's true you're the oldest millennial in the world."

The door opens and Justin looks at us, confused. "Is Cassidy okay?" he asks and honestly, that is probably the best thing the kid could have said.

"She's fine. We're not here for her. Is your mom home?"

"Justin, who is it?" Marjorie calls, walking out of the kitchen. She pauses when she sees us. "Oh, Leo. Hey. It's been so long."

Phoebe looks over at me, and I know she's thinking to herself, who is this beautiful woman calling this old man *Leo*? The mother of my daughter's boyfriend, that's who.

"Everything okay?" Marjorie asks, before introducing herself to Phoebe. "Okay, wow, two detectives in my house on the night of a full moon. Feels ominous."

"We're hoping you can speak with us, actually. Cassidy mentioned you may have given readings to the girl, Katherine Calloway, who has been missing for over three days."

Marjorie shoots Justin a look.

"Sorry." Justin shrugs. "But you're not a doctor; it's not a secret who you see or anything. Besides, everyone is kinda spooked over the girl going missing. Like, who could be next?"

"This is not a serial-kidnapping situation." Phoebe's tone is laced with caution and I hope Justin understands the severity of the case at hand. It may not be a serial killer on the loose, but a missing girl is urgent. "It is an unusual investigation, though," Phoebe continues. "That's why we're here — we need a better understanding of Katherine and we were hoping you might be able to shed some new light on the case."

"Justin," Marjorie says. "Why don't you go finish up dinner in the kitchen and give us a minute, okay?"

He nods, doing what his mom says.

"So, you heard about him and Cassidy?" Marjorie asks.

I run my hand over the back of my neck. "Yeah, guess they're all grown up."

Marjorie groans playfully. "Don't say that. I'm not ready for this to all be over. We should have had more kids. Prolonged the inevitable."

I shake my head. "I'm glad our kids can at least talk to us, tell us what's going on. Means a lot."

Marjorie nods slowly. "Speaking of kids, the girls from Glennmare, a lot of them do come here quite a bit."

"I never realized," I say.

"I think when they get some pocket money, they come visit me because, well," she shakes her head, as if embarrassed, "I think they miss their mothers and I'm like, a mom?"

"Interesting," Phoebe says. "I can imagine it's like seeing a therapist, getting a tarot reading and finding some direction."

"You would think they have counselors at the academy," Marjorie says. "But it sounds like they don't have anyone to talk to. The girls seem sort of . . . lost."

"Is that how Katherine seemed?" I ask.

Marjorie indicates for us to sit on the cushions on the floor in the living room that is also serving as her place of business.

"Honestly, Katherine wasn't like the other girls. She was confident in ways they weren't. She knew herself, entirely."

"The cook at the school mentioned she was the ring-leader of sorts, always planning parties for the girls, celebrations. That she was a good friend to them."

"I'm not surprised. She's singular."

"What do you mean by that?" Phoebe asks. "Do you have an example?"

"The other girls always came together, in little groups, eager, nervous, asking about love lives and lifelines, but Katherine had other things on her mind."

"Not only thinking about guys, then?" I ask.

Phoebe snorts. "Don't reduce girls to that."

Recognizing my ingrained thinking once she calls me out on it, I apologize. "You're right. I'm sorry. But what did Katherine want, then?"

"At first it was a tarot reading. She wanted the cards to tell her if what she was thinking about doing was a good idea."

I swallow, thinking of Wells Halifax. "Did it have to do with someone she was . . . seeing?"

Marjorie shakes her head. "No, it wasn't about a relationship. It was about an action. She didn't offer details, but it could have been about acting on something. But it didn't seem like that. It felt like she was already seeing someone, if I'm being honest. I told Frederick this earlier, that friend of Katherine's teacher."

"You spoke with Frederick Rooper?" Phoebe frowns. "When?"

"Today. He came around ten this morning, asking questions about his friend."

"Wells was a client of yours, then, too?"

Marjorie nods. "He was interested only because his students were. It was really thoughtful, actually. He was looking for more ways to connect with them. He teaches Irish Literature and there are a lot of oracle traditions that surround tarot. He was looking to make a curriculum around tarot to teach the history of it. He thought the students at Glennmare might really enjoy it. It seemed like he really wanted their validation, if I'm being honest."

Phoebe nods. "That sounds problematic. For a grown man to want young girls to like him. Did Wells strike you as, well, untrustworthy?"

"Not particularly, but, again, our encounters were more about history and origins. Actually, they were similar to my interactions with Katherine."

"Katherine was interested in the history of tarot?"

"Not exactly. After that first reading, where I pulled the Star card—" Marjorie picks up a tarot deck on her coffee table and begins to sift through it. She finds the card she is looking for and shows it to us. "This is the Star. It is a Major Arcana card and Katherine loved the imagery. I remember her looking at the symbols and wanting to know what each one meant."

"And what do they mean?" I ask, looking at the card. There is a naked maiden at the edge of a brook, drawing water. Stars surround her, one gleaming brightest.

"Well, for one, she is nude, which means she is comfortable in her own skin. The water she is pouring in and out of the jugs is a cleansing process. And it is also a card about time. She pours out water into the brook in the present time and is also pouring out a river that runs through our future days as well."

"And the star?" Phoebe asks.

"Well, it can be a few things, but Katherine latched on to the idea that it was guidance from a higher power. Like how the wise men were led by a star to the birth of Christ?"

"Is she religious?" I ask Phoebe. "How did we miss that?"

"I don't think she's particularly devout. But she was very curious about something specific . . ."

"What?" I ask, not backing down. I need all the information she might have. "Don't hold back."

"It's this ancient rite. That is what I think she wanted the affirmation for with the reading, because once we finished pulling cards she opened this book for me, an old one, and it had a description of this old Irish ritual for kings. She wanted to know if I believed it was real. If doing the rite would bring the man closer to his higher power. Closer to God."

"You're losing me," I say. "An ancient Irish rite?"

"Google it," Marjorie says. "It's pretty twisted."

"Google what, exactly?" Phoebe asks, her phone in hand.

Marjorie pauses before speaking. "The Knight's Rite."

CHAPTER 39. WELLS

Tippy doesn't want me to leave the cottage. "It's freezing, and dark out," she says. "Besides, Freddy will be back soon with dinner. And you need to be well rested before the trip to Seattle tomorrow."

"I know," I tell her as I wrap a scarf around my neck. I have a flashlight in my wool coat pocket. "But I need to take a walk. I've been cooped up inside for days."

It's clear she's annoyed, but I can't care. Curiosity drives me forward. All afternoon I have been picturing the moment in my dreams. The girls and me, in the cottage. I am hoping it recalls my memory. I am also thinking of other things. Other terrible things I can't stop imagining.

The note in my pocket reads:

Our dearest Wells,

We have two wishes. That you would no longer be stuck in the past and that our future has Kitty in it. Come to the old cabin at six o'clock tonight. We will be there, waiting. Willing to do whatever must be done.

Love,
The Girls

Whatever must be done? I clench my jaw, wanting to imagine pure and good things only, but instead picturing something much less restrained.

As soon as I step outside my cottage, I see a woman entering the home on the right. "Wells, how are you?" she asks, eyeing me warily. "I stopped by yesterday, but your friend said you were sleeping."

I press a hand to my head instinctively. "I'm so sorry, I've lost all memories of the last several months, and I'm hoping, well, I have a neurology appointment tomorrow."

"Right. Well, I'm Melinda Ellis. The math teacher, among other things."

It's clear from the way she's looking at me that she can see I have no idea who she is or how well we know one another.

She helps me out. "We've been friendly, but I think we were both busy this fall settling into our new jobs."

So we weren't that close, then. "You just moved to the island too?"

She nods. "A month after school started, actually."

"And what do you think of it?"

"It's been good until now. It's terrible, everything that has been happening. Your accident, poor Katherine, and now Duncan? Half the girls will be gone by the weekend."

"What happened with Duncan?"

Her mouth falls open. "I guess you haven't heard. He was arrested yesterday."

"Did it have to do with the girl?"

Melinda shakes her head. "Oh God, no. Though if it had been, at least we would have answers. It was over some money scandal. Evidently, he was stealing hundreds of thousands from the school."

I consider her words. "And the families are presumably upset."

"I think the missing girl thing spooks them the most," Melinda says. "It's all so strange. She was such a likable, popular girl. But also serious about her studies . . . It just doesn't add up that she would have walked away."

"Hopefully they'll find her soon," I say. "The detectives on the case seem pretty determined."

Melinda nods before opening the cottage door. "Glad you're feeling a bit better. And I hope the appointment tomorrow goes well. Keep me posted, yeah?"

"Of course. Good night."

I look at my watch. It's six already. Picking up my pace, I walk briskly toward the water before veering right, toward the path that apparently will deliver me to the cabin, hoping I am going in the right direction. The sky overhead is dark and it smells like rain is coming. The grass is damp as I walk over it in my leather boots.

My side hurts, but I took pain pills right before I left. I hope they kick in soon. With the flashlight directed on the path, I begin my descent into the woods, carefully choosing my steps.

Soon, the cabin is before me and I take a deep breath. I do not know what lies before me, only that the girls are connected to me in a way that scares me, in a way I crave.

Visions of them have filled my mind since the amnesia set in. Katherine naked, the girls surrounding her, the entirety of the cabin lit up with a light I can only describe as holy.

My body stirs in a way that it shouldn't. These are my students, after all. Aren't they? Or are they more?

And are my dreams memories, or just hallucinations? I pray it's the latter.

I deliberate for just a second before I pull open the dilapidated door of the cabin, and then I see them all standing there.

Four beautiful girls, dressed in long white dresses, hair floating down their shoulders, eyes turned to me. A majestic brown mare held by the girl with jet-black hair. To see the horse in this crumbling old cabin is a surprise and as I walk toward it, it backs up, spooked by me.

I look around at the girls, waiting for them to say something. Anything. When they do, it's more hostile than I was expecting.

"I'm Coretta, and, while I adore you," she says as if she has nothing left to lose, "if you did something to Kitty, I will kill you. I swear it."

"Coretta," the redheaded girl shouts. "What are you doing?"

"I'm telling him what he needs to hear. I need Kitty back."

"We all do," the tall girl with white hair says. "We all need Kitty. But we aren't going to find her in this cabin."

"I want to remember," I say to them, stepping closer. Suddenly I don't feel like their teacher, but more like their . . . ruler? It's almost as if I hold some sort of twisted dominion over them, but surely that's all just in my head.

The dark-haired girl jolts me from my thoughts. "We want to believe you're trying to remember, but . . ."

"But what?" I implore her. "Just tell me."

"But you were the last person to see her. She ran out of this cabin, sobbing, and you went after her."

"And then?"

"Then we went back to Glennmare, thinking Kitty would be in the dorm, but she wasn't. Somehow Johanna found you on the beach, unconscious. But knowing her, she was probably sneaking around, listening to us talk when we got back from the stables. She probably went on a mission to find Kitty herself."

"Then maybe she's the last one to have seen Kitty," I say. "Is that possible?"

The girls exchange glances, looks that say, yes, that is possible.

"What do we do now? Because Johanna hasn't confessed and you don't have your memories and I just want Kitty, she wasn't herself that night, hadn't been in a long time. But neither were you . . . we're all leaving tomorrow and I don't want to go without knowing she's okay . . ." Diane starts sobbing then, and I step forward, wrapping this waif in my arms.

"It's okay, we'll sort this all out. We must."

She is fragile and delicate, and I will do anything to stop her cries. I feel my body harden with desire. *Anything.*

"In your letter to me, you said you were willing to do whatever must be done," I say. "What do you mean? What were we doing here Friday night?"

"It was nothing like what you were doing during the yuletide festivities, that's for sure," Jolie says with a tight laugh.

"Tell me," I beg. "You have all the power here, do you see that?"

Bernie looks at me. "First time for everything, right?"

"What do you mean?" I ask. "Have I been misusing you in some way?"

"No, not you. Kitty. She's the one with the power. She's the one in charge."

"In charge of what?" I ask.

Coretta presses her lips into a tight line. "In charge of you."

I shake my head. "What? How?"

"She cast a spell over you," Bernie says. "Not literally, though I wouldn't be surprised if she did that too. You were in love with her. Obsessed, really."

"Was I in love with you four as well?" I ask them. "Because I keep having visions . . . thoughts . . . I see us, here . . . together . . ."

Coretta's eyebrows lift curiously. "Do you want to be together?" she asks. "With us? With all of us?"

I clench my jaw. They must see my need, the desire growing within me, for them all. I tug at my hair, tormented with what I want. I remember Iris. So young, innocent, she looked at me with devotion and it was what I craved, what I always wanted. Attention.

My parents never gave it to me. My brother certainly didn't. None of us ever saw eye to eye; they didn't understand that knowledge was freedom. They were fine being stuck in their provincial lives. Which is why I was so determined to leave home and never look back.

It was exactly what I did. I focused on my classes because I had nothing else going for me, got scholarships, went to Yale and changed my story. I found two friends who were looking for a cause, for someone to love. I let them choose me.

Until, of course, we let our familiarity trick us into thinking we should push our friendships further, deeper. Sleeping with Tippy was the beginning of the end, for both Freddy and me. There is no coming back from that.

And then, I suppose I fled to this island and found new devotees. New ways to garner the attention I so deeply crave.

It sounds garish, when I say it like this, so simply, but it is the truth. It is not my fault, really, for being the sort of person that draws people close. I learned to choose my words carefully, to draw attention to the parts of myself that would endear me to others. And mostly, I asked questions and then listened to the answers. If more people simply did that, they would have a much simpler time getting through life.

I look at the four girls standing here before me. God, I want to run my hands through their hair and tear off their dresses, I want them plain and simple, in their entirety.

I wonder, though, have I had them before? Did they bring me here to spark my memory of an act we've already shared? My gut tells me I have crossed a line before. But what line was it?

"I want you to be satisfied, all of you. I want—" Just as I am about to offer myself to their lust-filled eyes, Bernie cuts me off. "Do you smell that? It's gasoline!"

We spin around, the horse neighs, and the back wall of the cabin begins to smoke. I take control. "This way, come on." I press them toward the door as the already sunken roof begins to creak, falling in as we run into the clearing in the woods.

Diane screams. "Oh God, I don't want to die!"

"We're fine. It's okay . . ." Jolie's tear-filled eyes give little confidence to her words.

Outside we can see the back of the cabin on fire, but the night is wet, rain is falling, and the fire dies quickly as heavy raindrops snuff it out.

There is a distinct smell of gasoline in the air. "Someone did this," I shout. It wasn't wood burning, it was gas. "Who would do this? Who knew we were here?"

"We didn't tell anyone, but someone could have followed us?" Bernie says, huddling with the girls. The horse's reins tightened in Coretta's hands. The horse whinnies, scared, and I step toward her, running my hands over her silken hair. "It's okay, girl, you're okay. Let's get you home."

We leave quickly on foot, Coretta walking the horse back. I stand with the girls in the stables, unsure who is most visibly shaken from the fire. I can't believe what I was tempted to do — desired — before it began.

I look at the girls, frozen in their sheer dresses, their coats lost in the old cabin. "Will you be okay getting inside? Would you like me to come talk to someone?"

Coretta shakes her head, tears rolling down her cheeks. "No. We wanted your memory to return so we could find Kitty. And that didn't happen. I don't know how we thought it would. I suppose we're always hoping for things that won't happen."

The girls take one another's hands, walking past me.

"Why was I obsessed with Katherine?" I shout after them.

Coretta looks at me as if I'm a fool and right then I feel like one, and more. "Because Kitty was not the sort of person you could say no to. Even if you tried."

CHAPTER 40. FREDDY

When I get back with Thai food, Wells isn't here.

"Tippy?" I knock on the bathroom door.

"Just a sec, drying off from a shower."

I look at my watch, knowing I was gone a lot longer than I said I would be. It's been two hours, maybe more, since I left the cottage. But I had to sit at a bar for an hour drinking whiskey to get the nerve to make the call I had to make.

As I am unloading the bag of food, Tippy joins me, dressed in an oversized sweater and flannel pants. Her hair may be wet, but she looks bright-eyed.

"Where is Wells?" I ask her.

She shrugs. "Right after you left to get dinner he decided to go on a walk."

I frown. "And you let him wander off alone, at night? Tippy, he isn't well. He is on medication. He—"

She cuts me off. "He's a grown-up. He doesn't need me babysitting him, Freddy. Besides, what took you so long?"

I reach for a bottle of opened red wine and pour a glass, offering it to Tippy. She accepts and I pour another for myself. "I called my father."

"What? Why?"

I take a drink of the Cabernet before answering. "I am quitting law school."

"My God. I did not see that coming. And what are you planning on doing with yourself?"

I smirk. "You know, you sound just like my old man."

"Fair. Sorry." She lifts her wine glass. "To rash and irreversible decisions!"

I laugh. "Well, it is reversible, you know. I could start over anytime."

"So why the break? Can't hack it?" She gives me a mock pout.

"Don't tease me. It's not about hacking anything. It's about wanting something different for myself."

"And what, pray tell, is the plan?"

"I'm buying a boat."

She nearly spits out the wine. "Freddy, be serious!"

"I am serious. Enough about me, what did you do while I was gone?"

"Since Wells was gone, I was a little bored; I started organizing his hall closet."

I lift an eyebrow. "Okay, is that a code word for snooping?"

"Are you going to judge me if I say yes?"

I pop open a box of noodles and then split a pair of chopsticks. "No. It's overdue actually; things are not adding up."

"Tell me about it. Those girls from his seminar were here earlier today. I was in the bathroom and I don't think he realized I heard them, but it's more than a little odd. Who goes to their teacher's bedroom window?"

"It's not appropriate, especially considering his apparent fondness for Katherine."

"What do you mean *fondness*?" Tippy asks, reaching for a container of rice.

"I met this woman in town, Marjorie. She reads tarot and Katherine came to see her. Apparently Katherine was in love with someone."

"You think it was Wells?" Tippy glances at me. I shrug, giving my reply. "Okay, even if this girl was infatuated with her teacher, Wells would never do something so reckless."

"Explain Iris, then."

"Iris was different. She wasn't in high school for starters."

"Sure, but she was his student. She was in love with him and he used it to his advantage. He told me she was all innocence — that he knew he could get anything he wanted from her. And it wasn't a one-time thing."

"Please, let's not rehash the reason Wells slept with her a second time." Tippy groans. "This is all too much. I hope the doctor has something helpful to say tomorrow."

"So what did you find in the closet?"

Tippy's eyes grow to saucers. "Right, okay, so it's kind of intense. But it also validates your theory about the relationship between Wells and that girl."

"Validates, how?" I set down my food and follow her to the hallway, where she pulls a large box from the closet.

"This was shoved in there. It's full of unusual items. Honestly, we should call the detectives but . . . it's *Wells*. I don't want any more trouble brought to him."

My heart pounds as we kneel on the hardwood floor and open the box. We begin sifting through its contents and I grow more agitated with each passing second. There is a long lock of brown hair tied with a black velvet ribbon that truly terrifies me. "What the fuck is this?"

"I don't want to know," Tippy says. "And look, these notes." I begin to read.

WH,

Tonight, after the yuletide festivities, we shall have our own union. The first of its kind.
Yours, KC

* * *

WH,

The flowers you left for me . . . remind me of how you plucked my . . . oh, you know what I mean. Stop blushing.
Yours, KC

* * *

WH,
> *Impossible to sleep without you.*
> *Yours, KC*

"Okay, God, that is plenty," I say, setting the notes aside, feeling sick. Is Wells a predator? Did he seek Katherine's affections knowing she was an innocent girl? These notes don't give me much faith in his morality. "What's that?"

"A set of some sort of oracle cards, but not ones I've seen before."

"They look hand-drawn," I say, taking a few of them from the pile next to Tippy. "Is that some Irish symbol or knot?" I show her.

"I think so. But, actually, are these tarot cards or just a story told in drawings?" I see what she means as she begins to line the set of cards on the floor, in a row. They are numbered and depict a sequence, a story.

"You're the writer, what is it saying?"

"I'm not an artist, though," Tippy says. "It looks like a white horse in the center of a gathering."

As we look through the cards, we see a man in a crown doing unspeakable things to the white horse, before what looks like decapitating it and cooking it in a huge pot.

"This is one convoluted story. Maybe it was a class project? Some ancient Irish myth."

Tippy nod. "I bet you're right. That makes sense. All this is probably a class project."

"Locks of hair are not a project, Tippy."

"I know, but . . . the card, the notes, the hair . . . and at the bottom of the box is . . ."

"What?" I ask, my stomach dropping. I reach in and take the last object from the box. Its wicked blade glinting in the light, offering a fresh horror.

"Oh God," I say, just as the front door opens.

It's Wells.

"What the fuck are you doing?" he shouts upon seeing me with the object in my hand.

Why is there a machete here?

"You tell me," I say, standing, facing him. "Tell me what all this is, because something doesn't add up, Wells, and we need to know what you've done."

He begins to tug at his hair, clearly agitated. "Dammit. Why can't I remember?" He is growing hysterical. My own heart pounds, trying to reconcile my friend with the man before me. He has kept plenty of secrets, taken advantage of me dozens of times — and I've let him. The idea of losing him was too much. Until, of course, I did. Should I have come here at all? Let myself get entangled once more with a man who knows how to wield his power in ways I never have?

Now he grabs the cards on the floor, reading the notes. "My God, what have I done? Who am I?"

"I don't know, Wells, but I'm scared," Tippy says, crying now, too.

"I need to remember," he shouts. "I need to remember!"

"Where have you been?" I ask, still holding the knife. "You left hours ago. And you smell like smoke."

"There was a fire at an abandoned cabin." He starts shaking, gripping the hallway walls for balance. "I was with the girls. If the fire hadn't started, I think . . . I was going to do something horrible. I can't trust myself. I don't know who I've become since I moved here. I don't even want to think what I would have done with those girls if the fire hadn't started."

His words sound hollow to my ears. He has compromised himself before — with Iris, with the lies surrounding his origin story, with the way he allowed me to give and give to him for so many years without truly thanking me. Instead, he paid me back by sleeping with Tippy — the one person I always longed for.

Tippy is still crying, reaching for Wells' face. "Stop saying that, it's not true. You are a good person, Wells, just a little lost is all. But we all are, aren't we? In our own ways?"

"I would have taken all of their innocence," he continues, berating himself. "But, truly, I may have already done such a thing. I can't trust myself. Months of my life are missing!"

Goodness knows I've explained away Wells' actions before. We all have looked past terrible things we have done in order to move forward.

Still, his words are a shock, and his admissions of desire both enrage me and renew my loyalty. He is not trying to hide anything, even the darkest parts of himself, and it makes me love him all the more.

CHAPTER 41. THE GIRLS

Wells just left us, the fire at the cabin killing whatever fool-ish plan we hatched. Now, we stand in the stables, reach-ing into a barrel for apples, feeding them to Violet, Petunia, Gardenia, Tansy and Iris. We kiss them, nuzzle their ears.

We're frozen and dizzy with thoughts, with harbored resentments and fears. We never stand in such silence, not knowing who is who, and what is to become of all of us. Tomorrow three of us are leaving.

We hate it. All of us. We want to rewind time. We remember Marjorie's three-card tarot spreads — past, pres-ent, future. None of the readings predicted this. That we would be facing one another in a dimly lit stable, blood coursing through our hearts and keeping us alive even though we are all more lost than ever.

"Kitty always knew what to say." Jolie laughs. "We always said there was no leader, but we were full of shit. Kitty was in charge of us. And now she's gone and who are we really?"

"No one is in charge of me," Coretta says. "I'm done following. I thought that this last year proved that I was strong and resilient, but it's a joke because I rely on you all for everything. We allowed Kitty to control us. We think as one — what would we have done tonight if that fire hadn't forced us to stop? We would have—"

"Don't say it," Diane says. "We wouldn't have."

"Why wouldn't we?" Jolie asks. "Kitty moved us to do the unthinkable once, even though we didn't want to. And tonight, she wasn't there to push us but look at us, we pushed ourselves."

"We wouldn't have had some wild orgy with Wells Halifax, in the freezing cold," Bernie shouts. "Would we?"

"We were acting like Kitty," Diane says. "But she was always so much larger than life. I always felt so much older with her around, like I could become the person my future self might be . . . but the truth is, I'm not ready . . . not ready to face the world like Kitty is able to."

"This time it wasn't Kitty making us do these things — she is gone and we were willing to do this! What does that make us?" Coretta asks.

"Monsters, maybe?" Jolie says, her tone sharp. "Part of us wanted to sleep with him, part of us didn't. But it's because the last week has been so confusing, so messy. We don't actually love him. It was the idea of him. Of someone choosing us."

The words silence us. Would we have given Wells anything he wanted tonight, even if it meant we were his second choice? On second thought, maybe we are his first choice now, since he can't even remember who Kitty is.

"I need to eat something," Coretta says, giving Gardenia a final kiss.

We walk through the back door, into the kitchen, dazed. Of course, we want it to be empty, we want to raid the pantry unwatched, but Johanna is here.

She is always here.

"Oh my Lord, look at you, all of you frozen to the bone." She rushes to us, urging us to sit, but we don't have the energy for her. We never have.

"Stop." Bernie's voice is flat. Heavy. "Don't coddle us."

Johanna presses a hand to her heart. "I know it's been a long few days, and then with the headmaster leaving like that. A true shock, I'm sure. I bet you loves could use some hot cocoa — let me make a batch."

"We don't want hot chocolate," Coretta says. She pulls open the door of the fridge and grabs a roasted chicken. After removing the plastic wrapping, she begins to dig into the meat with her hands. Eating as if she is starved. We all are, actually, and we circle her, the chicken before us. Grabbing knives from the drawer, we reach for wings and thighs, ripping them from the carcass.

"Girls, this is unseemly." Johanna looks at us with disgust. "Get a napkin, plates, what are you thinking?"

Thinking? *Us?* We laugh.

We look up, our mouths full. "We're eating," we say, our eyes dull and our minds numb. What have we become? Our truest selves? Finally free? The false bravado of the last year, of all our lives, fading away at long last.

Who are we without ribbons in our hair and love in our hearts?

We are depraved. We aren't girls at all. We never were.

"I must ask you to stop, let me help make you a proper meal—"

We turn to her, this pathetic woman who has wormed her way into the lives of the students just to make her own life interesting.

With knives raised, we sneer. "We can make a proper meal," we say with blood in our eyes. "We've done worse already."

CHAPTER 42. WELLS

The hallway seems to spin as I sink to the floor. They've gone through my things, and what they found stuns me to my core.

But should it? I tell myself the story that I am a good, honorable man.

Am I?

I've abandoned my family, lied about who I am; I ran when things got difficult with Freddy and Tippy. Not to mention the dalliances I've had all my life, the ones I've kept locked up, away.

They think when I slept with Iris it was a simple affair. But it was more than that. It was nights in candlelit rooms, where I would run a knife over her thigh. Causing her to bleed. I told her to do the same to me. I wanted to feel something. To become more than a man. I wanted her to need me, more than anyone else. It was late-night interludes, where I would tie her up to my bedposts, make her beg, and more. I wanted her to need me.

I thought if I pushed her to the very edge, she would cling to me for dear life. Instead, she left me, saying she wanted to experience college without strings attached, wanted to have fun with her friends. That I was too demanding.

The last time I slept with Iris, after Tippy rejected me, it wasn't because she wanted me. Although it was mutual, I was of course taking advantage of the power imbalance. I knew that and did it anyway.

I never told my friends such stories. That this box of evidence tells me a clear story — I am not good, no matter how hard I taunt people into believing I am. I know what I am. Trouble is, who else does?

Tippy and Freddy join me on the floor, both with wide eyes, staring at me as if I'm a madman. Am I? Freddy is the one holding a machete.

"What are you doing with that?" I ask him.

"It's yours. You want it back?" He holds it out to me, his eyes dark and furious.

When I don't reach for it, he sets it on the floorboards. "What is all of this?"

Tippy pushes a cardboard box toward me, skittish, as if I've scared her. Of course I have — I am scaring myself.

"I'm sorry for snooping in your things. I just, I don't understand what's been happening here, and thought maybe there was something in the house that would help us understand. Help you get your memory back."

Her level of generosity toward me makes me want to weep. She is still here, after everything. After I pushed her away earlier today. After she tried to make amends. She is here, plans to drive me to the doctor's tomorrow, by my side through thick and thin, and I am sitting here, angry that she's looked in my closet?

"What did you find?" I ask, shoulders falling. Side aching. Knowing her end is near. Maybe it is for the best.

"Here, just a sec." Tippy stands and goes to the bathroom, returning with the bottle of pain pills and water. "Need something stronger?"

"I do," Freddy says, walking to the kitchen. He returns with a bottle of scotch and three tumblers. Pouring them out, he hands us a round. "To . . . to . . ." He can't finish the toast; neither can I.

Tippy smiles. "To your boat."

"Boat?"

"Freddy here gave his pops the finger and decided to buy a yacht."

Freddy laughs. "Not a yacht. A sailboat, and there was no giving the finger. It was actually a civilized conversation. Turns out my father respects me more for saying what I want."

I consider this. For as long as I've known Freddy, he has had a tenuous relationship with his father, but, as an outsider, I've always seen it in simple terms. They are too similar to recognize one another. Maybe choosing different paths will allow them to appreciate one another for who they are — and aren't.

Sentimental thought considering I may be a pedophile.

"Katherine is eighteen, correct?" I ask, feeling sick.

"Yes, but why in God's name are you asking?" Tippy demands.

"Her roommates have told me I am quite obsessed with her."

Freddy looks disgusted, his lips curling, tossing me something. Hair. "She's eighteen," he says. "So are all those girls she plays dress-up with."

"What the hell is this?" I ask, gesturing at the pile of notes and locks of hair.

"Your obsession's cuttings."

Nauseated, I drop the clump of hair. "I don't want to know why I have it saved." Tears sting my eyes as I drop my head back.

"Do you know what these mean?" Freddy asks. He hands me a pile of cards, with intricately drawn illustrations. "Look, I know your memory is gone, but they might mean something anyways. They're numbered," he explains. "And they tell a story, we assume."

I lay the cards out, one by one, examining them as I do, wanting something to click, to make sense.

It does.

"This is the telling of an ancient Irish rite, when a king would become sovereign over a land."

"By fucking a horse?" Freddy says, aghast, then nudging Tippy. "Sorry."

"It's fine." She exhales. "It's all a bit overwhelming."

"Perhaps it was something I was teaching in my seminar? I taught Irish Literature this fall. Maybe it was an assignment of some sort?"

"That is the most reassuring thought of the night," Freddy says.

"Though that king does look like you, a bit at least," Tippy says. "The dark hair, his stature."

"It's a drawing," Freddy says, taking the card she is holding. He frowns. "Though to be fair, the resemblance is there."

He holds the card for me to see.

"Please," I protest. "I don't want to read into this any more."

"The notes, though, are quite damning," Freddy says, tossing them at me. "If we were going to call the detectives over anything, it would be those."

I take the papers and read them over, feeling more dread with each word.

Impossible to sleep without you.

I look at my oldest friends. "Did you already call the cops?" I ask, terrified of their answer. "Please, tell me the truth."

"No," Tippy says softly. She takes my glass and fills it with another inch of Scotch. "We're still holding out hope that you'll remember."

I toss the Scotch back, all at once. "Thing is, Tippy, at this point, I think it might be better to forget."

CHAPTER 43. BERNIE

We leave the kitchen wordlessly. How can we speak again? Ever? Our words have too much power, our thoughts too.

Disgusting and still half frozen, we walk to the shared dormitory bathroom. At our lockers we pull out our things. Robes and slippers and soaps and salves.

With water on as high as it can possibly run, we wash off the last few months. Scrub it away with washcloths lathered in lavender. We disappear, each of us, under our own shower head, facing our own horrors.

We must have you home. My mother's voice rings in my ears and right now it is all that I want. To be with her. So badly. But I wonder if it's even possible, after the last few days, to go back to normal? Return to my old life and become whole somehow, with a mother who never understood me and a father who only ever tried to fix me, a life that's always been tortured with privilege, with having everything I want and more and still none of it being enough.

My back burns. I want the water to wash away my sins, scour out my horrific thoughts.

I would have slept with him if he let me. How would I have stopped it when I haven't even confessed to the detectives what happened Friday night?

When I am with my friends, I tap into the darkest parts of myself.

Do all girls do this, or is it just me?

I've been jealous of Kitty all this time and pushing it down, down, down. Away. Pretending I was okay but how could I be okay when I feel like a monster is inside me and I just want it gone?

The pills never worked. The guys never worked. The therapy never worked. Why would I think a school in the middle of nowhere could have cured me?

I look at my friends, crying under the spray of water, waiting, just waiting for the sound of a siren, the finality we all crave. Just please God let someone find Kitty and let this be over. Our hearts are equally broken, we've picked up the shards. But I don't want to fight with pieces of glass.

They are why I thought I was better, thought I was finally, for once in my life, enough. The girls.

My girls.

Diane and her hysteria. Coretta and her cravings. Jolie and her attitude. Kitty and her control.

Me and my magic.

Except what magic was it really? A deck of cards can't decide my fate no matter how much I cling to the idea that this life is out of my control.

It would be easier, I think, if I didn't hold my own destiny in my hands. Maybe that's why I was so willing to hand mine over to Kitty. She understood power, she was able to wield it.

Me? I shuffled cards, aching for answers.

I turn off the water, wrap myself in my robe. Slippered feet move me down the hall. Alone, I enter our room, pulling out my most favorite deck. Tears in my eyes, desperate for a sign.

I shuffle, I pull.

I gasp.

But I shouldn't be surprised.

The Death card is in my hand. I look out the window, looking for her.

She is already gone. I know it.

CHAPTER 44. FREDDY

While I felt momentarily buoyed by my conversation with my father, now a cloud covers me. Wells is breaking apart; Tippy is cradling him in her arms. And a chill has set in. Even if Wells has nothing to do with Katherine's disappearance, he does have something to do with her. Something that will alter his life, forever.

He has been my friend, though, and I can't turn my back until I know for certain.

"It's going to be okay," Tippy coos. "I'm here, and I'm not leaving. I love you, darling."

I look at my stepsister, appalled at her words because I know her voice too well. Usually, her inflections are practiced, but now they are real in a way that catches me off guard. She truly loves Wells? Even though she knows the pain she's caused me, him — she still is declaring her devotion. At a time like this. Why?

I break away from them and enter the guest bedroom where Tippy and I have our things. I want, suddenly, to be done with my friends, forever. I want to take a sailboat around the San Juan Islands and maybe write a goddamn book, not the one Tippy is always going on about. I want to write a story that actually gets finished.

Thinking of Tippy and her novel, I wonder if she is lying about her progress. In her leather tote bag, I see papers and a laptop case. Knowing it's snooping but remembering that she felt all right doing this with Wells' things, I give myself permission to look in her bag.

What I find as I flip through the papers is a receipt that falls out, tucked between pages of scribbling.

My stomach drops, sinks really, to the bottom of the sea and I find myself sitting down on the bed, in the empty room, alone, confronted with the facts. Finally. Fragments of the facts at least.

"Freddy, dear," Tippy calls from the hallway. "We need more wine. Can you grab us some? Can't exactly get up, we're having a bit of a moment."

I reread the receipt.

Tippy was not in Oregon at a writing retreat for the last few weeks.

She was here, on this island.

And I have proof. In my hands is the receipt from an extended stay, paid for in cash, at the Whidbey Inn.

CHAPTER 45. WELLS

Freddy exits the bedroom with fists clenched. I try to get up from the floor and focus on whatever his problem is, but my head aches and my body is sore.

"Just sit." Tippy cuddles me as if she has forgotten altogether that I told her we were through. But now, actually, as she presses my head to her chest, I realize this is warm and soft and safe and this is where I belong, with her. Maybe I always have and should have fought harder when she pushed me away last summer.

The past, though, is just that. Past.

Now, Freddy is grabbing wine in the back of the cupboard, uncorking a bottle as he stalks toward us. "Here," he says to Tippy. "You don't need more of it, but suit yourself. You always do."

"Why are you being so cruel?" she asks him, standing. She reaches out her hands, helping me to stand too. "I am just here being a good friend, trying to support Wells because he's in a real mess."

"I know about his mess." Freddy sneers at us both. "And God forbid I get in the way of your unyielding devotion to our dear friend."

I must have missed a portion of their fight. My head throbs even harder. I take the wine and pour a glass, hoping the libation will numb the pain at least.

While they are arguing about their parents and this damn boat, I drink a glass of wine, then, needing something stronger, I pick up the half-downed Scotch and drink from the bottle. There, finally, I feel something.

Walking toward them in the kitchen, I offer them the bottle. Drunk beyond reason, I've lost my filter. "You know, those letters aren't the worst of it. We ought to call the police now. I can turn myself in because tonight . . . oh God, tonight. That was the worst of it. My plan, what my body wanted. You know what my plan was?"

"I don't think I want to hear," Freddy says.

Feeling both free and utterly cornered, I tell them the truth. "I was going to sleep with those girls. I had it all mapped out in my mind, I could practically feel their innocence in my hands. I kept dreaming about doing it, the last few days."

"God, Wells," Freddy shouts. "Cut it out!"

"I know, it's horrific, isn't it?" I laugh sharply. My limbs numb as my heart. "But I didn't. Didn't so much as touch them. But I wanted to. It's why I met them at the cabin in the first place."

"You were in a cabin with the girls? Tonight?" Freddy asks.

Tippy looks at him. "Does it matter? We have no proof that Wells has done anything wrong."

"Why would you meet them in a cabin?" Freddy asks. "What good could possibly come of it?"

"Good?" I smother a twisted laugh.

The good would have been me, with them.

My dreams would no longer simply be fantasies — they would be reality.

I can't say that aloud, of course; some things are too private to tell even your closest friends. Some desires too forbidden. Though Freddy knows plenty about taboo. He slept with his stepsister how many times? I truly don't want to know. I am not the deranged one here.

179

CHAPTER 46. JOHANNA

When the girls leave the kitchen, I look at the chicken carcass discarded on the counter. A rage I haven't felt in years boils within me.

How dare those entitled, spoiled girls talk that way. Just like how the headmaster dismissed me earlier today.

Me, a pillar of strength for this school. Me, a woman willing to keep any secret, to squash any rumor, to protect this place.

And they all treat me like a fool, a joke. A reason to roll their eyes.

I thought the girls loved me, I did, but now I see it was all a stupid game to those privileged children with their la-di-da ways.

I'm done with it. With them. I will not stand by and be treated like the trash that needs to be taken out.

I can take it out myself, thank you very much.

Picking up the knife on the butcher-block counter, next to the platter that the girls feasted upon, I consider my options.

There is really only one.

CHAPTER 47. DETECTIVE LEONARD ABBOTT

Knocking on the cottage door, I feel a chill set in. Glennmare itself is shrouded in the night sky, the grounds cold and unapologetically detached from the rest of the world.

Phoebe coughs. "This feels off."

I am about to agree when the door to the cottage opens. The petite woman, Tippy, whom we met yesterday, answers, her black bob swinging as she pulls the door closed behind her. She steps onto the porch, greeting us. "Wasn't expecting anyone so late," she says. "Everything okay?"

Her voice is a whispered hush.

"Is Frederick here?" I ask.

She frowns, confused. "Frederick?"

"We had a few questions for him."

"Questions?" Her eyebrows lift before she presses her lips in a firm line, as if resolved. "Actually, no. He left a while ago for a walk. But I heard his car leave the driveway, so I'm not actually sure where he went."

Frowning, I take her in. Her eyes are red. Her arms are wrapped around herself, to stay warm.

"Do you have any idea where he might have gone?" Phoebe asks.

Tippy shakes her head. "No, I'm surprised he'd be out so late, considering we have such an early morning."

"What is happening in the morning?" I ask.

"Wells has an appointment with his neurologist in Seattle. He is already in bed, and actually I should be getting to bed myself."

"Of course," I say. "I don't want to keep you. But will you let Frederick know we are looking for him? I tried to call, but he didn't answer."

At this, Tippy frowns again. "Why do you need to speak with him?"

"It's about the investigation."

"What does he have to do with the missing girl?"

"Nothing, we just had some questions for him," I say.

Tippy nods. "Of course, I will tell him as soon as he returns."

We thank her for her time then turn to leave. I turn back to her. "And I hope the appointment goes well tomorrow."

Tippy smiles softly. "Me too."

Phoebe and I walk away and, God, at this moment, I wish I still smoked cigarettes. Not finding a more solid answer to where Katherine has gone is killing me.

"Should we wait?" she asks.

I nod. "Let's walk around and see if he comes back in the next half hour or so. It's after nine. Nothing will be open on the island for much longer except the bars."

As we begin walking along a stone path around the exterior of the academy, I point to the kitchen door at the back of the academy. It's been left open a crack.

We walk toward it, seeing a flicker of candlelight. As I pull open the door to see if anyone is inside, I reach for my gun.

On the kitchen floorboards, over a hundred years old, there is a puddle of red, someone lying face down in the center of it.

"Oh, shit," Phoebe mutters as we enter the historic academy.

There is a bloody knife next to the body.

CHAPTER 48. WELLS

When Tippy comes back inside, I hand her a glass of Scotch. I can tell she needs it. She's practically shaking, it's so cold. "Tell me, what did they want?"

"It was the strangest thing," she says, before taking a sip. "They wanted Freddy."

"Freddy?" I shake my head. Regretting the movement immediately as my head starts to throb. "Whatever for?"

"They didn't say, but it can't be good. It's late — why would they be questioning him anyways?"

"No idea," I say slowly. "But it worries me. Why was he so keen to leave?"

Tippy exhales, pacing the room. "I don't want to think about it," she says. "I just . . . I want to go back to before. To the days at Yale when we were all together and happy and there were no hurt feelings."

"I know," I say, pressing my fingertips to my temples, feeling like a knife is dragging across my skull. "Damn, it's worse than it was two days ago, as if this headache is trying to crack me in two." I don't add that visions are piercing my mind's eye.

"Do you need water? Or to lie down?" she asks. "Or food? We hardly touched the takeout."

Tears spring to my eyes and I groan, finding a seat at the table. "Maybe it will pass," I say as Tippy hands me a carton of rice. I push it away. "I feel ill, Tippy."

"All right," she says, carrying it back to the counter. "How about a cool flannel on your head?"

She begins to soak a washcloth under the faucet, and, as I watch her, I am confronted with a memory — a vision, at least. One of the girls — Diane? — with a rag in her hand, on her hands and knees. Blood everywhere. "Dammit!" I moan, panicking.

"What is it?" Tippy asks, offering me the wet rag. "What's wrong?"

"I think . . . oh God, Tip, you'll hate me . . . I can't . . . I see them. Her. Kitty."

"A memory?" she asks. "That's good, Wells. Don't fight it."

"You don't understand." I squeeze my eyes shut, though it does nothing to erase the vison. "I see her covered in blood . . ."

"Don't say that," Tippy commands. "Look at me, Wells. Don't. You are innocent. You have to be."

Crying, shoulders shaking, I realize I am a monster. The man I wanted to believe I was, he doesn't exist. "The girls must be covering up a murder."

It's then that Tippy loses patience. "Don't say that. No one can hear you talk this way!"

"But if it's true . . . oh, Tippy, I have always been worse than you wanted to believe me capable of. I must have killed her!"

"Stop, Wells!" she demands, but I can't stop sobbing, shaking. Panic courses through me. The blood was everywhere. The girls were washing it away.

"Listen to me — stop!" she shouts. When I don't cease to blubber, she draws back a hand, smacking me right across the face. It catches me so off guard, my chair tips back, and as I fall my head catches the edge of the table behind.

I roll to the side in agony, lying on the floor, lights flashing in my eyes. Tippy crawls to my side, hysterical. I press my hand to my head. My hair is coated in warm, thick, metallic blood.

But that is not the worst of it.

The fall may have done more good than damage.

Because, suddenly, I can remember.

CHAPTER 49. FREDDY

The moment I realize Tippy has been playing me this whole time, I know there are bigger questions at hand.

Namely, why is Tippy lying about where she has been?

I leave the cottage needing to think — and find myself driving into town, toward the Whidbey Inn.

Maybe it is reckless, rash — to jump to the conclusion that Tippy is involved with whatever happened the night Wells lost his memory, but she has been lying.

On the paperwork for the stay at the inn, the person checking in was Eleanor Everest. The name she used to check in with is not lost on me. It is the name of the main character of the novel she has long claimed to be working on.

But there was no writing retreat on the coast. Has she been writing at all or was it just a ruse?

For so long I have held a candle for her, wanting what Wells had. Tippy and I were classmates long before our parents married. The crush I had for her began when I was fifteen. Her style and humor matched my own. Her blue eyes drew me in every time she looked my way.

I never meant to fall in love with her. But once I did, my own father foiled my plans of ever asking her out by proposing to her mother first.

Then I was living with her. The girl I longed for was across the hall in our Manhattan mansion, in her pajamas and bedhead, and, when she looked at me, I forced myself to look back without showing my true feelings. My desire.

But our friendship grew; we became inseparable and while I tried to keep a distance between her heart and mine, I soon came to see that my feelings were reciprocated. Both of us were forced into purgatory now that we were stepsiblings.

Anyone who was close to us could see we were more than friends, different than siblings. Our relationship was unnamable, hormonal teenagers wanting what they couldn't have.

When we were young, I nearly kissed her once. It was winter break, in Switzerland, and it was late. We'd been drinking mulled wine and sat before a fire and our fingers brushed, and, God, I wanted her then. There. Forever. But as my lips drew close to hers, we stilled — hearing a door down the hall creak, our parents pulling us back to reality.

We were related. By marriage, sure, but it was enough of a taboo to keep us apart.

When we decided on Yale, we knew we needed a third person in our dynamic because the tension between us was fraught. Wells Halifax was the missing piece to our triangle.

Now he may very well be what has severed us, forever.

I see the sign for the inn and I turn right, into the parking lot, not sure what I hope to find, but in my gut I know there will be something here.

Parking my car, I think of last summer. Tippy coming to me when I finally pushed my longing for her far enough away to not think of it constantly.

We were at the house on the Cape, alone. Our parents and Wells were coming the next morning, but we'd driven out together. She wore a white-and-blue-striped button-down over her bikini. I was in the kitchen, looking for gin. She came up to me, wrapping her arms around me from behind, her cheek against my back. I was twenty-four but felt fifteen all over again.

The first time we made love it was fast and out of nowhere, and I wanted to slow down time, to hold on to this feeling, to find a way to make her mine. It was my deepest wish for so long, and, finally, she was in my arms, kissing me and making me remember why I loved her for so long.

Then, before she could be anything more, be the one I had longer than a night, I learned about her and Wells sleeping together.

No matter why she slept with me — to get back at him or over him or to make him mad — it was all about *him*.

It was never, not once, about me.

Did that stop me from letting her back in my bed after Wells moved to Whidbey? I wish. It would make me feel strong, to come across as the one in control.

But I wasn't. I was alone and I wanted what I couldn't have before and I was jealous, insanely so, of Wells' and her relationship, entangled as it was.

And when I learned he asked for a commitment over the Fourth of July and she refused — I also felt hurt on his behalf. How dare Tippy refuse our dearest friend? Why break Wells' heart and then mine in turn?

Now, as I walk the gravel path toward the hotel lobby, I take in my surroundings, turning on the flashlight on my phone. There are several cabins dotting the property and a large inn overlooking a cove.

Tippy stayed here for two weeks. She hasn't been back since Wells was helicoptered to the hospital. She met him there, brought him home.

Wells must have known she was in town. Had they rekindled their affair and didn't want me to know? Was Tippy unable to tell me in fear of hurting me all over again?

Dammit. Maybe it is as simple as that — Tippy and Wells are in love and Tippy can't tell me they're back together because she doesn't want to upset me.

And here I am, arriving at this old inn, looking for what? A clue? Some proof my friends are out to get me? A reason to pin everything on Tippy because she chose someone else?

As I walk up to the front steps a man around my age comes round the corner. "Can I help you?" he asks, holding open the door for me.

"I, uh, was looking for a friend. She is staying here," I lie.

He gestures to the bundle of wood he's carrying. "I was just getting the fire in the lobby going. Give me a sec?"

"Of course," I say, watching as he adds a few logs to the large firebox.

He expertly strikes a match and lights some crumpled newspapers buried under the kindling. Satisfied, he wipes his hands on his work pants and then turns to me. "So, what did you need?"

"I was hoping my sister might still be checked in; she isn't answering her phone."

He frowns. "What's her name?"

The lobby tells me this inn built from logs is over a hundred years old. It is quiet, and there is a leather couch flanked by comfortable chairs, perfect to curl up in and read. Folk music plays through speakers, and in the far corner there is a bar where a handful of guests are gathered. It is quaint and nostalgic of a time long gone. In some ways, similar to Glennmare. Except the academy is full of Victorian relics. This place looks fit for the loggers and miners of the Pacific Northwest.

"Her name is Eleanor Everest," I tell the man as he walks over to the check-in desk. He taps a tablet, then looks up at me.

He pauses before speaking. "I'm not comfortable giving out information about guests."

"I'm her brother. And no one has heard from her since Friday," I fib. "I am going to the police next."

"The police? I don't want cops here. It will scare people staying here."

"Look, she's already paid through this week." I run a hand through my hair. "That's odd, right?" I ask, wanting something — anything — to hang onto. "Is she in one of the cabins or the main building?"

He exhales. "Considering she's not here, I guess I won't get fired for telling you. But she rented the Penn Cabin. It's the farthest out on the property, toward the lagoon."

"And has it been cleaned since Friday? Look, I am not trying to cause trouble. I'm scared that perhaps something bad happened to her."

"Bad?"

"Look, can I go to the cabin and make sure nothing is amiss? It's my sister."

His shoulders relax then, no longer thinking I might be here for trouble. "You're really her brother?"

I nod. "Yes. That's why I'm so worried. Look," I say, pulling out my phone and opening a photo album from this past Christmas. "Here we are, around the tree."

He nods slowly, taking it in, then his eyes widen. "Is she missing?" he asks. "Because there's another missing girl on the island."

Feigning shock, I lie. "Yes, she is missing. That is why I want to be sure she isn't in the room . . . that something hasn't happened."

The reality sinks in. "The cabins only get cleaned on Tuesdays and Fridays, so no one has been in there. So, if something . . . shit. We should go look, huh?" he asks.

I nod, relieved that he is helping. "Yes, please. Then I can go to the cops."

He grabs a set of keys from a box behind him. "I'm Dale, by the way."

"Frederick," I say as we exit the inn. "Have you worked here for long?"

He nods. "Three years. My uncle owns this place. I restore boats on the side."

"Boats?" Our feet crunch on the gravel as we wind through the property. "I'm in the market for one myself."

"Yeah? We should talk." He points ahead of us. "Here's the Penn Cabin."

The lights are off, madrona trees surround the cabin, and there is no sign of anyone. Still, I tell Dale we need to look inside.

He nods. Stepping to the door, he knocks. When no one answers, I call out the name Eleanor, knowing it is impossible for Tippy to be here. I left her with Wells, in the cottage, where they were getting sloppy drunk and increasingly panicked.

"I'm gonna unlock it — you cool with that?" Dale asks.

"My sister would understand," I say, expressing my worry.

But my worry is for more, for worse — for everything.

Dale inserts the key, twists the knob, and immediately we move to cover our noses to block the smell.

"Damn," he says, covering his mouth. The foul stench of something rotten overwhelms us and we step back. "Dude, I don't think that's a good sign." Dale groans.

Stepping forward and flipping the lights on, I move through the cabin. There is no one in the living room or the kitchenette. The single bedroom is empty.

As I push open the door of the bathroom, though, I hear myself crying out in shock. A body lies in the bathtub, bloated and nearly beyond recognition. The tub is full of murky red water, and the floating body of a woman dressed in white.

Dale comes up behind me and curses. "Is that your sister?" he asks.

"No," I say, bile rising. "It's Katherine Calloway. The girl who has been missing for three days."

CHAPTER 50. JOHANNA

There are footsteps in the kitchen, but I can't make out who it is from the dim candlelight. I close my eyes, the blood draining from my wrists.

It's over.

The last thing I want to be is pathetic and after seeing the girls' looks of disgust, I knew I was always a joke to them.

I wouldn't let them have the last laugh. Headmaster Duncan, too, seems to think I am a fool.

I tried. I thought it would get better. It hasn't. I thought these girls were like my new daughters, that they needed me. But now I see I'm just a joke to them. I'm meant to be with Matilda.

Taking my own life ensures they will weep for me, tell stories about how good I was to them — because I was. I made them meals and kept their secrets and washed the academy clean with my discretion.

But all that work got me here, on the cold kitchen floor, bleeding out.

I thought it would be more painful, using the kitchen knife to cut open my veins, but it was oddly easy. Though, I've always been the sort to follow through once I've set my mind to something.

Just like how I set my mind last Friday. I saw Kitty walking up from the beach. It was a gloomy night. The wind howled. She passed the stables. She wasn't alone.

I didn't tell the detectives any of that. I'm sure they dismissed me just like Duncan did, I saw them making eyes at one another, insinuating I was nothing special. If they treated me with less condescension, I might have told them the truth of it.

Kitty was walking with a woman I had only seen once before, a few days earlier, while in the grocery store.

Kitty got in her car, willingly. They left Glennmare together.

Why didn't I want the detectives to know this? Because like I've said before, I am good at keeping secrets. And I told them about the pregnancy, didn't I? I am not cold-blooded, I just know not everything needs to be said.

If I could do it over again, I would have kept my mouth shut about Kitty's condition, but God knows those detectives were champing at the bit for something. I figured one morsel would be enough to get them off the girls' backs. Now I see that Kitty may have been playing me the entire time. Was she even pregnant? I will never know.

Someone is near me, warm fingers on my throat, but it's too late.

My chest no longer rises and falls. At long last, on the other side, I can finally find my daughter.

The sad truth is most girls are lost. And by the time they are found, it's too late.

CHAPTER 51. DETECTIVE LEONARD ABBOTT

Pressing my fingers to her neck, I check for a pulse, but it's clear we are too late. Johanna, the cook, took her own life.

"I've called this in, Leo," Phoebe says. "An ambulance is on its way." There is no time to waste and I must push past my need to process the bloody scene before me.

My phone is buzzing in my pocket, but I want a moment. I swallow, realizing it's all coming undone at once. With a curt nod, I answer my phone.

"Detective Abbott? It's Frederick Rooper. I've—"

"I was just looking for you. You met Marjorie today?"

"Uh, yeah, but, you need to come here. Now." His voice is scratchy, broken up, and I realize he is crying. Hard.

"Where are you? At the cottages?"

"No, no. I'm at the Whidbey Inn. In a cabin. I, uh, I found her."

"Found who?"

"Katherine Calloway."

His words take my breath away. "What the hell? Is she—"

"It's bad. She's . . . oh God, it's so . . . she's . . ." He is no longer coherent.

"I'll be right there. Hang tight."

Getting off the phone, I fill Phoebe in. "Oh hell." She looks at me, knowing that whatever we find at the cabin won't be good. "You go to the inn and I'll stay here and wait for the ambulance."

"You sure you're okay here, alone?"

But we already hear sirens on the property. Above us the floorboards creak as the girls wake, talking. Racing down the steps.

"Oh my God!" A young student in a white nightgown shrieks as she steps into the kitchen doorway.

"Stay back." Phoebe's words are firm, keeping everything under control.

I step around her toward the back door. "I'll call you as soon as I know something."

In the car, I race over with my lights on full beam. It's pitch dark, the February night heavy and cold, and I don't slow for anything as I drive. Frederick found Katherine.

At the inn, I park and then jog over to the cabins. "Frederick? It's Leonard!"

"Back here," a voice calls out. Dale, the manager, and a lifetime resident of the island, finds me on the gravel path. "She's in the cabin by the lagoon," he explains.

"Is Frederick there?"

Dale nods. "Yeah, he might still be puking, though. He may be some fancy city boy, but he did the right thing. Got me to open the cabin."

"Oh, thank God," Frederick says upon seeing me. He stands on the porch, looking like death — pale, as if stricken with images he can't unsee. The cabin's lights are on, illuminating him.

"Where is she?" I ask.

"The bathroom," he says. "But to warn you, it's—"

I cut him off. "I've seen it all."

But I haven't. Not really. Because when I enter the cabin, the smell hits me with the horrific truth. Katherine is dead. Has been dead for days.

A girl, gone.

A teenage girl — someone's daughter. My mind goes to Cassidy, praying she never falls in with anyone who would lead her to this.

The curtain is drawn around the porcelain clawfoot tub. I step toward it, biting back the foul odor by clenching my jaw. The curtain is white, with ruffles on the bottom — delicate — and I close my eyes, praying that what is behind this screen is anything other than the desperate truth. But the truth is inescapable, and it always catches up.

She lies in a pool of water. Bloated and waterlogged. Her long brown hair swimming around her. A fly has landed on her cheek, resting. The single Edison bulb hanging overhead offers a soft glow to a scene that deserves a spotlight.

Katherine Calloway is dead, a girl barely grown, daughter, friend, student. Possibly a mother.

Stepping out of the bathroom, I collect my thoughts — two dead women in one night.

Outside I call the dispatcher, notifying them that we need EMTs and a coroner at the inn. With dread I know we need to call her parents. First, I need to talk with Dale and Frederick.

We stand on the porch, and they explain to me what happened from the moment Frederick set foot on the property.

"I didn't think there would be anything like this in the cabin," Dale says. "How did she even know Eleanor?"

"Eleanor?" I ask.

Frederick pales under the light of the moon. He tears at his hair, his eyes red. This guy doesn't want to tell me the truth.

"What do you know, Frederick?"

He exhales, as if in defeat. "It's Tippy's cabin," he admits. "She was staying here under an alias. What kind of brother am I to tell you that?"

I clench my jaw, refraining from exposing my thoughts. Tippy was involved. "You are a brother who knows right from wrong, it seems."

Frederick, wiping the tears from his eyes, explains what happened at the cottage, how he felt a prick of concern and rooted through Tippy's bag, finding a receipt for an extended stay here. "It seemed impossible. She told us she was at a writing retreat on the Oregon coast. But she was here, this entire time."

"Why lie?" I ask.

At this, Frederick blanches. "Tippy doesn't let go easily. Especially not of Wells."

Frowning as sirens roar toward the inn, I tell him it's time to join me for a drive. Clearly there is more going on at Glennmare than any of us knew.

CHAPTER 52. WELLS

After I fall against the kitchen chair, the memories come at me, hard, quick. And as I register the relationship I had with Kitty, it's impossible to reconcile myself with the man I must truly be.

The evening of the yuletide festivities, the girls in my seminar were giddy. While part of me wished Kitty had more discretion, there was something powerful in the way the girls saw me.

They didn't see me merely as a professor, or as Tippy did — as a man who could be disposed of. They didn't see me like Iris did, as a stepping stone to someone better.

No, they saw me as capable, wise, powerful.

They saw me in the very best light and I can admit to finding a distinct allure to that level of control. I had never been so unanimously adored and it was intoxicating. I didn't want my admirers to be let down. I wanted to give them reasons to love me even more than they already did, but I carried a nervous energy, a fear of letting them down.

Glennmare was decorated resplendently; everyone wore velvet and satin, suits and smiles. Traditions matter here, and an old-fashioned Christmas felt right. As if we were in a scene of *Little Women* or a Charles Dickens novel — candles were lit, orchestral music played. The eggnog helped, as did the alcohol-laden fruit cake, and every faculty member and student was in attendance.

At the white elephant gift exchange, I received a drawing of the academy at sunset by a sweet sophomore named Lenora. Somehow Kitty managed to walk away with the present I brought — a leather-bound copy of *Alice in Wonderland*.

When the partygoers began to disperse, I left for the abandoned cabin. Kitty told me to meet her there, for our promised night. While she was finally of age, I knew I would have to have a conversation with her about boundaries. I didn't want to lose her affection, but I also knew there was only so far I could go.

She tempted me in ways no one ever had before.

And she was the opposite of Tippy. Kitty never tried to reshape herself to fit — she was free to be herself, entirely. Tippy on the other hand was keenly aware of every situation, how she might appear, how she was being perceived. It made me pity her, that sort of insecurity. It made me love her too, but that was beside the point. Once I asked her for more than secret rendezvous and she refused me.

For so long I used Tippy's insecurity as a blanket, protecting my own self-doubt. But Kitty couldn't care less about anyone else. She was a magnet for me, and for all the other girls in my seminar. Her ability to both draw one close and push others away was a lesson in confidence. And I craved it.

Her idea was a terrible one, even if I so desired to give her the world. Kitty deserved to receive the gift she wanted for her birthday: me.

And I wanted to be alone with her. She had stirred something in me that no one had in such a long time.

But I also knew I couldn't sleep with her.

Once she joined me in the cabin, my resolve changed. She looked so young, so innocent. Her friends were so close by, as if on watch duty.

She stepped into the cabin, looking as divine as ever. I heard the other girls outside, giggling and joking, mentions of passing the bottle traveling toward us. "We should leave," I told her, already regretting coming this far. "The other girls will be cold out there."

Kitty shook her head. "They have warm coats, cigarettes and vodka. They are fine. Besides, keeping a lookout is their birthday gift to me. Are you scared?" she asked.

Her question made me feel small, and all I wanted was to be valued. If I cowered, she would see me as I saw myself. Nothing. I had the power, for this night at least, to feel like more than that. To feel alive.

Clenching my jaw, I knew I was going to have to make a choice, and, once I did, there would be no going back.

The fact she was a virgin made the situation quite simple, really.

Even if I wanted her innocence, wanted her bound to me, it wasn't an option.

"You haven't even told me I look pretty," she said, lowering her chin, lifting her eyes.

"Katherine, you know I think you are beautiful."

She smiled demurely, then jutted her chin toward the blankets and pillows in the corner. "They even brought us bedding."

"I can't sleep with you," I whispered, stepping toward her, knowing I would be breaking her heart.

"Yes, you can," she murmured.

"I would lose my job, my—"

"No one will ever know. Besides, they won't even have proof. We are alone, Wells. It's our secret."

"I can't," I whispered, my words catching in the cold. I wanted to hold her close, feel the warmth of her skin. Forget the moral implications of this choice and instead lose myself in her acceptance of me.

"But it's all so perfect. It's my birthday, we just had the party, we're all alone. My best friends adore you, nearly as much as me." She practically burst with joy. "I want this night to be perfect. And it is! So perfect I can practically taste it."

She could easily float away in a fantasy; it happened plenty of times — like when she suggested to the seminar class that we take a midnight horse ride to celebrate the full moon or find a rowboat and let ourselves get swept away to sea. And I found it fascinating. She set the current, the pace — like when she crawled in my bedroom window a few weeks earlier, hungry for me, and begged me to take her virginity, right then. "I can't bear to wait any longer!" She stood before me looking like starlight, like a wish fulfilled, but the agony of her unmet desire flooded her face. Her eyes pleading with me, her hands on my cheeks, as she tried to make me understand what she craved.

Oh, I understood.

But I refused her then — having drawn a line in the sand. Now, here we were again and I didn't want to disappoint this darling creature.

And while I had boozy eggnog at the party, and shots of whiskey before that, I wouldn't let the alcohol sway me now.

I took Kitty in my arms. "Happy birthday," I whispered in her ear, wanting desperately to suck her lobe, to lower my mouth to her bare neck. Wanting to move to the makeshift bed, to lift the hem of her velvet dress.

"I'm sorry," I told her instead.

She whimpered, tears in her eyes. "You must." This girl was used to getting what she wanted.

"I won't."

She paused, looking up at me, her skin glossy. "Don't you love me?"

"Yes, I love you." I looked down at her adoringly. Her body was pure and holy and mine if I wanted it. Instead, I stepped back.

Finally, she sighed, realizing I wasn't going to give in. "I am going to let them believe we did anyways."

"Who?"

"The girls."

"Why?"

She shrugged. "I want them to believe I get everything I want."

"No." I hated this idea, the last thing I wanted was to lose my job. I'd already lost Tippy and Freddy. "I can't have rumors spreading about my ethics."

She smirked. "Oh, Wells. Why are you such a poor sport?"

Leaving the cabin in the dead of night, I would be lying if I said I didn't regret my choice a little.

Kitty was otherworldly and in a different life, I felt as if she would have been mine.

* * *

After the agony of the night wore off, I questioned my sanity. The next week I was back at it, berating myself for wanting her innocence. And then every time I began to despise the man I was, I would catch a glimpse of her, looking over her shoulder, her eyes on me. And everything would go still, the world once again made right.

For a bit, it was enough to be spun up in Kitty's world. Perhaps I was living out a fantasy and even though I pushed away from what I knew she was truly asking for — to sleep with me — every time I saw her all I wanted was for her to be enraptured by me. I wanted her devotion, and I had it. At least I thought I did.

Then, a month or so later, things changed.

It was her fixation with the Knight's Rite that was the beginning of the end. For us, and all the girls.

By then, Kitty had a growing obsession with what she read about in the school library, and that we discussed a handful of times in the seminar. When we discussed it, though, it was always in the context of learning.

She wanted to take it further. She always wanted to take everything further. And it was as if my rejecting her in the cabin made her want to double down on her newest scheme.

"We should do it," she said one wintery afternoon in early January, in my seminar; we sat in a circle on our wooden chairs. "We should perform the ritual."

Jolie snorted. "You want our teacher to take a horse?"

I smirked, thinking she was wanting to be sensational, not serious. "Enough, Kitty. You need to let that go."

She said she thought it was dramatic and beautiful. "You would be the king and it would prove your loyalty to all of us."

We laughed, and she scowled. "Are you truly saying no to me?" she asked.

I paused, leaning my elbows on my knees and looking at this devious girl. I spoke plainly. "I am saying no, Kitty. No one is having sex with a horse, no one is slaughtering a horse, and, certainly, no one is going to eat the meat of the horse."

She crossed her arms. "I was meaning metaphorically. We could act out the ritual just to see what it would be like."

Bernie, with her tarot cards in hand, gasped. "Look what I just pulled." She flipped the Knight of Pentacles toward us. The horse on the card was black, not the white mare the Irish lore told of, and this rider held pentacles. "The pentacles in tarot represent money," she said. "But maybe for Kitty they are a talisman, a symbol of her deepest desire."

"Put the cards away, Bernie," I said sternly. "We need to drop this."

"We could do it Friday night," Kitty said, her eyes sparkling.

"Why are you so into this?" Coretta asked. "It's ridiculous on all accounts."

"The kings and clansmen didn't think so," Kitty said. "And like I said, we can make it a play. A performance. We never do anything around here."

Coretta snorted, her eyes flitting between Kitty and me. "You do plenty."

I tensed at that, the words hitting closer to home than I liked. Clearly Kitty had let them believe what they wanted about her and I, even though I told her not to.

"That was over eight hundred years ago. Things have changed," Jolie said. "Now, can we get back to the lesson? I was wondering what everyone thought about chapter fourteen?"

Kitty screeched. "God, none of you can be counted on. I ask you for one thing. One! And you say no." She grabbed her bags and stormed out of the classroom, tears on her cheeks.

She slammed the door, leaving us with a thrumming silence. "What was that about?" I asked my four remaining students.

"She's been really emotional all week," Diane told us. "It's like she's not herself."

"Every day she has a tantrum," Coretta said. "I love her, but she is not stable."

Bernie scoffed. "Kind of harsh. So what, she's dramatic? It doesn't mean there's something wrong with her."

Something was shifting in this group of friends. The girls rarely argued, or even exchanged tense words. It was one of the things I loved about them all — they didn't feel like teenagers, like children. They were more mature than that.

Weren't they?

"Has she mentioned this rite outside of the classroom?" I asked. While I was close to the girls, we didn't spend suspicious amounts of time together. I always assumed her friends were the liability, not Kitty herself. Now, I was not sure. The last thing I could afford to have happen is for her to get angry and ruin me.

"She was talking about it yesterday," Coretta admitted. "God, I hate talking about her when she isn't here but . . . she was telling me about her plan when we were in the bathroom. Said the reason the rite felt so powerful was because it cemented everyone's devotion for one another. Like if you sacrificed a horse together, you would all be so stricken by what you'd done, everyone would remain loyal, forever."

"And that's what she wants?" I asked. "Absolute loyalty?"

"Makes sense," Jolie said. "Her parents sure aren't loyal to her. Didn't even call on Christmas. So she wants to create her own family, her own circle."

"You don't prove loyalty by breaking the rules of society, by partaking in illegal activities," Diane said, then her cheeks went red and she looked away from me.

"I thought she wanted to *act* it out, not actually do it," Bernie said.

"Kitty doesn't do anything halfway," Jolie said.

I felt a gnawing in my belly, an understanding that Kitty didn't just let things go.

Jolie's words sent a jolt of panic through all of us. "Crap," Bernie said, shaking her head. "We need to . . . I think you and Kitty should . . ."

"I know," I said, taking control. "We should put a stop to this. All of it. We are going too far. Even our friendships are too entwined for teachers and students."

But my words felt flat, hollow. Untrue. I was so in love with the idea of Kitty, of her needing me, that I wasn't ready to let it go either.

The girls looked at me with eyes of sorrow. "I don't want anything to change," Diane whispered.

But it was too late for wishes like that. Kitty had already. And we'd let her go off alone — now nothing was ever going to be the same again.

CHAPTER 53. DETECTIVE LEONARD ABBOTT

"I'm fine, Dad, I promise. I have the doors locked and put a frozen pizza in the oven. I'm going to watch a movie then go to bed, okay?"

"All right. I love you, sweetheart."

"Dad," she says, laughing. "I love you too. Go catch the baddies, all right?"

I end the call as I pull into the Glennmare parking lot. Phoebe meets me as I turn off the ignition.

"God, she's really dead?" she asks. Before calling Cassidy to check in, I called her on my way here from the inn, explaining things. She said the ambulance had just left with Johanna's body. The entire academy was lit up with the horror.

"Everyone awake?" I ask as we walk toward Wells Halifax's cottage.

"Seems like it. The timing for arresting Duncan wasn't ideal, but at least it means most of the girls are already leaving for home in the morning. This place is nothing but bad vibes."

"We need to arrest Tippy, bring her into the station, get the whole story from her there," I say as we stand outside the small cottage.

"You hear that?" Phoebe asks. There is shouting inside but we can't make out the words.

"Guess Tippy was lying when she told me they were going to bed," I say.

"She was lying about everything," Phoebe replies. "Why do you think she has Katherine's body in her cabin? Do you think Tippy killed her?"

"It looks like she drowned, there were no wounds on her body, so I'm not sure where the blood came from. I can't know if she was forced under or not. The autopsy report will confirm it, though," I say.

"This isn't going to be pleasant," she says as we step forward. Phoebe knocks on the door.

Inside, it goes quiet. We knock again. "This is the Oak Harbor Police Department. Open up, now."

Wells opens the door. Pale-faced, aghast, holding his side. His voice slurs, he holds a half-empty bottle of Scotch. "You're here, I presume, to detain me?"

I frown, looking past him.

Tippy stands still, eyes wide. "Shit," she whispers.

Wells turns to her. "It's okay, Tip. I can remember everything now."

CHAPTER 54. WELLS

None of us wanted to Kitty to be angry. We loved her, all in our own way. She made Coretta feel seen, Bernie feel accepted, Jolie feel singular, Diane feel like a princess. She saw what everyone desired, and gave it to them with kisses and smiles and hugs. She knew how to read people and, God, it was a gift to be read like that.

After the uncomfortable conversation in the seminar, she wrote each of us a note, inviting us to the cabin.

> *Dearest Ones,*
>
> *We will meet at the old cabin Friday night at nine o'clock. Wear white, bring candles, I've made oracle cards and have the supplies we need. The only thing missing is you, of course. We can prove our loyalty to each other is deeper than all the rest, once and for all.*
>
> *Bound to you forever,*
> *KC*

I, for one, knew I would go. Not just out of curiosity, but also out of a deep need to make Kitty happy.

I didn't want her even more unhappy with me, and clearly not sleeping with me upset her. She wanted more. She wanted more of me. But I knew I needed to clear the air — make sure the other girls knew I never slept with Kitty, and that our seminar class was crossing the lines of appropriate. I wanted them to love me the way we all loved Kitty, but I also didn't want to become a monster.

I was scared it was already too late.

I rode my black stallion to the cabin, tying him up when I arrived. Next to it was the only white mare from the stables. My stomach fell, wondering how much acting Kitty was actually planning on.

I heard something — someone — in the woods. "Who's there?" I called out. I heard heavy feet moving in the distance. "Who is it?"

I frowned, turning back to the cabin. Opening the front door, I saw the interior of the cabin was circled in candlelight and, as I entered the familiar space, I realized I was the last one to arrive.

"Finally." Kitty smiled at me. "I knew you would come." She walked toward me and then, standing on her tiptoes, pressed her perfect lips to my cheek.

I inhaled her sweet scent, not wanting the moment to end, but also aware that her roommates were staring.

She stepped back, revealing the rest of the cabin to me. In the center, drawn in thick salt lines, was a pentagram. In the middle was a giant cauldron, hanging over a steel fire pit you might see outside in the summer.

"What is all this?" I asked.

Jolie shrugged. "I don't know. What's with the secrecy, Kitty?"

"Just a moment." Kitty beamed, clapping her hands, then leaving the cabin.

Diane took the opportunity to express herself. "I think she's not herself. She's off . . . frantic, or manic . . ."

"What were you saying?" Kitty asked, returning with the white mare. "Sorry, I had her tied up outside until we needed her."

"Needed her?" Bernie asked. "What do you mean, need?"

Kitty closed her eyes, a serene smile spread on her face as she led the horse to stand over a large brown tarp. "It is time for the Knight's Rite."

She looked angelic then, her hair around her shoulders, the candlelight illuminating it, her words sending a chill through the cabin.

"Stop it," Jolie said with a tight laugh.

"No," Kitty pressed. "The pentagram has five points, one for each of us."

"There are six of us, though," I said with trepidation.

Kitty smiled. "And you, my beloved, will be in the center."

"With the boiling cauldron of water?"

Her eyes seemed to turn dark as never before, as if she was another person altogether. "Don't ruin this. Can't you all see how wonderful it will feel to know we are all in this together, a family, forever? And Wells will make the ultimate sacrifice for us, proving his love as a father."

"A father?" I asked, stepping toward her, thinking she needed me to rein her in. The word 'father' somehow how struck me harder than the request she made. She did not want to act out the Knight's Rite — she wanted us to perform it, literally.

Coretta was crying, Diane bit her nails, Bernie shuffled her tarot cards — but we were beyond that sort of magic.

Kitty was in desperate territory; it was clear by the way she looked at us, as if we were her possessions. Speaking for myself, I knew I was hers.

"Yes," she said, placing her hands on her stomach. "I'm pregnant."

There was a collective gasp as the statement sank in.

"You're pregnant?" I asked, shocked. "But it isn't mine. You know that, Kitty. Don't you?"

"Yes, it is," she said, looking directly at me, her eyes brimming with tears. "I am pregnant with our child and if you refuse me this, I will have an abortion."

Jolie laughed sharply. "Kitty, you can't make ultimatums like this."

"Or put your decision for your body on us," Coretta added. "It's not fair."

Kitty petted the mare, looking away from us. "I have the money for the abortion. Johanna gave it to me. I can go right now, if you'd rather."

"Go where?" Bernie asked.

Kitty shrugged. "Seattle. Though I don't want to. I want to have this baby, Wells. But the choice is yours."

"You shouldn't have a baby at all, Kitty," Jolie hissed. "You're a child yourself."

Her words sent a chill through me. "Kitty, we never slept together. This child isn't mine."

"Yes. It. Is!" She stomped toward me and outside I heard a crash, my stallion neighing.

"Who is that?" she asked, spinning on her heels, opening the front door, stepping outside.

Jolie looked at me. "Wells, this is nuts. You realize she wants you to have . . . *relations* with that horse."

Diane spoke up. "When she first told us about the rite, she said it was the ultimate act of devotion. Is that what she's after?"

Kitty ran back inside the cabin, looking frantic. She stepped toward her friend, taking Diane's hands in hers. "Exactly. It may be extreme, but it is also grand."

"Grand?" Coretta whispered, shaking her head. "No . . . it's more barbaric than anything."

Kitty pressed her lips together, anger flaring. "Do you want to leave, Coretta? Because if you do, it means the rest of us will be bound together forever. Without you. Is that what you want?"

Coretta shook her head. "No, I love you all so much. You're my whole world. It's just, I'm scared."

"You don't have to do anything," Kitty said. "Except, well, have the meal."

"By meal, you mean the horse meat after you've chopped it all up and cooked it in that cauldron?" Jolie presses a hand to her head. "Am I losing my mind here? Because this is insane, Kitty!"

Kitty exhaled slowly, leading the horse to Wells and offering him the reins. "Have I gone mad? I'm afraid so, but, let me tell you something, the best people usually are."

She was quoting *Alice in Wonderland*, the book she'd been gifted during the yuletide festivities, and, when she spoke those lines, my heart was sealed to hers, regardless of whatever might come next.

The other girls were in various states of duress. Part of me wanted to go to them, calm them down, but Kitty held me back. Her eyes fixed on mine.

"Jolie, Coretta, Bernie, Diane, you should leave now. I will calm Kitty down and get her back to the dorm," I explained with clarity.

"You're staying? Are really going to do this?" Coretta asked me slowly.

"Of course not," I said, shaking my head with disgust. Kitty was a liar, and all these girls her pawns. I was a pawn too.

Why was I out here alone at night? All so these girls would give me attention? It's pathetic. I'm pathetic.

Kitty shrieked. "Yes, you are. You are all doing this!" She lifted the blade of the machete and spun, pointing it to us all. "You can't leave or I will make you pay."

The noise outside felt like a crash.

"Someone is out there," I repeated.

"It's just Eli," Kitty said, weaving the blade. "He wanted to come tonight and I said fine. I thought Wells would be too weak for the act, but thought Eli might be brave enough for it."

"You want Eli to perform the Rite?" Diane asked, her mouth gaping open in horror. Kitty didn't want to play make-believe. The cauldron and the horse were here for a reason.

She had lost her mind.

"Who is Eli?" I asked, feeling lost.

"The man Kitty gets to buy her booze. She sleeps with him too," Jolie said.

My eyes widened as a man about my age stumbled into the cabin. He was waving a bottle of whiskey. "Damn you, Kitty, you little whore."

"Excuse me, sir," I said, stepping toward him. "You can't speak to her like that."

"Why not? It's the truth." He was slurring.

"We need to go, all of us," I said, not wanting the girls here with this drunk man.

"No!" Kitty shrieks. "Eli can be our sacrifice. If you are too weak to kill the horse, we can put him in the cauldron."

She stepped toward Eli, pointing the machete, forcing him to the ground. He stumbles over the tarp and she jabs at him.

"Damn, you cut me," he growls. He reaches for his arm where she stabbed at him. Blood is on his hand.

"Stop, Kitty, I love you, but this is madness," Bernie said. "Before moving here, I was alone, and now I'm found. Seen. Loved. But this . . . this is beyond mad."

Kitty smiled with her eyes wide. "Then it sounds like you've made your choice. You don't truly love me."

Kitty and Jolie locked eyes then, and I saw a balance shift between them, watching as Jolie tried to keep her power from Kitty.

Maybe if we hadn't spent so many months separated from the rest of the world or if we hadn't been living at Glennmare without families we wouldn't have agreed.

But we were living in a distinctly unique universe where bonds strengthened faster, deeper, and more fully than in the real world.

The girls began sobbing as they realized that there were limits to what one would do for the person they loved.

It was something they knew before; their own families had exiled them. But they thought their sisterhood was stronger.

Turned out, it wasn't.

I never thought myself a hero. Not even a good man. I was flawed from the beginning. Before Yale, where I lied my

213

way into Freddy and Tippy's hearts, I was a fraud. As a child I always wanted to be someone else. Wanted a different life,

I never acted without selfish ambition. Until now.

Perhaps that made me heroic after all.

The girls shook with unease, faces twisted in hysterics.

"No," I said. "Stop, Kitty, you've lost your mind!"

"I haven't lost anything." She stomped one foot to Eli's chest and pulled the stack of oracle cards from her dress pockets, handing them to Bernie, who began laying them out on the floor of the cabin. "We have to do each step for it to be completed. For this rite to finish."

"You're scaring me, Kitty," Diane shouted. She never raised her voice. "This is too much."

"And if I don't stop, what will you do? Tell the headmaster Wells slept with me? That I'm having his child?"

"I didn't! And you aren't!" I shouted, but the girls weren't listening.

Diane shook her head, lost. "I don't know. Yes. I mean, they'll know soon enough that you're pregnant, right?"

"What kind of friend are you, Diane?" Kitty asked. "I thought we were like sisters, the five of us. We made promises to one another, to be there, through thick and thin—"

"You are taking that out of context a bit, don't you think?" Jolie asked. "Kitty, get a hold of yourself. We can go to the doctor, see the nurse. Maybe you need your medication—"

Kitty screeched. "Don't tell me what I need! I'm not going to take anything while I'm pregnant. Do you think I am a monster?"

The girls shared a look, an understanding.

"Have you been off your meds?" Diane asked more quietly, the bravest of the girls.

"That has nothing to do with this," Kitty said. "This act," she pointed to the oracle cards, "is about devotion."

"Kitty, listen." I decided to lie, realizing the most important thing was leaving this cabin with everyone — with every animal — alive. "We can leave together. You and me. Make a life. Leave this all behind."

"Not until you show me you truly love me," she said. "How much you love me," she added, eyes blazing, her body tense, fists clenched. She seemed ferocious, carnivorous. Like she was out for blood.

"We can all leave now, Kitty," Jolie pleaded. "We can go to the kitchen and make hot cocoa and—"

Kitty turned to them with obsessive determination. "No, we are already here. We will finish this!"

CHAPTER 55. KITTY

Before anyone can stop me, I pull a gun from my pocket.

"Where did you get that?" Coretta screams.

"Same guy who buys me booze. Not Eli, the other one. Though he doesn't know I took it. He went in the store and I looked through his glove box. Lucky, right?" I hold up the .45 caliber gun. It is heavy, loaded. Cold.

I look at Wells, taunting him. I know it isn't nice, but I love how malleable he is to me.

"What the hell are you doing?" Wells asks. "Kitty, this is too far."

"And this is for us all." I point the gun between the horse's eyes then turn to point it squarely at Eli. He is the father of this child within me, though it doesn't really matter.

Wells would take on the responsibility of raising this baby. I know he loves me, even if he is scared.

"I had sex with Eli. The baby's his," I tell them. "So I've already performed the first part of the rite." I smirk. "Now we just need to kill him, chop him up, cook him, and—"

"Stop," Wells screams. "Kitty, put down the gun!"

"Or what?" I ask, grinning and pointing it between Eli's eyes.

It's harder than it looks — the sacrifice, the act of shooting. But it is a powerful feeling too. One of absolute control.

And that is what I'm after.

"Don't." Eli is screaming too. "Please, Kitty, I love you."

Wells moves to stop me, but it's too late.

I pull the trigger, the bullet hits right between his eyes, ripping straight through, just as I wanted.

Eli's head explodes, blood splatters everywhere, on all of the girls. They scream, pushing at me, telling me I'm mad, that I've lost my mind, and so what if I have? There are worse things than being true to oneself.

Blood pours from Eli's head, his body limp.

He is our sacrifice, and for that I am grateful.

I turn to my lover, then to my dearest friends. A smile on my face. "We did it."

"We did nothing," Jolie yells.

Coretta tosses her hands in the air, exasperated. "Except stand here and watch you kill that man!"

"Don't ruin this moment with your tears." I press my palms together, my heart full. "We are joining together in this—"

"No. We aren't joining anything," Bernie says. "Kitty, you've got to get a grip. We have to call the police!"

"We love you, we will try to protect you, like sisters should — but this, Kitty, we can't," Diane begs. "It's gone too far."

"No," I say with righteous indignation. "You have to trust the rite." I hand Wells the machete. "Butcher him."

"That isn't happening." Wells looks at me as if I'm a stranger.

Am I?

I feel outside myself, free like I've been craving for so long. I know my mind is playing tricks on me. Two weeks ago, when I realized I was pregnant, I stopped taking my medication. I had to. I didn't want to hurt the baby.

And now . . . now . . . they are crying in the cabin, sobbing really, and I hate them for it. They are my best friends, and they look at me with disgust. But maybe they are just disgusted with themselves. I know I am disgusted with their weakness.

Of course, actually holding the gun and doing the deed was more difficult than I anticipated. The mare neighs beside us, shaken up by the gunshot. The mare should be grateful, though, that we let Eli take the bullet. One day I will tell this baby of his biological father's ultimate sacrifice. This baby will understand our devotion.

But everyone in this cabin is a quitter. Even Wells, the man I thought would do anything for me, said he won't do the rest of the rite.

I can't trust any of them anymore. I need a moment to think, to breathe — the impact of the metallic bullet still thrills me, but to what end? Wells says he is done.

I leave them hysterical in the cabin, stepping into the woods for air.

"Kitty." Wells runs out behind me, grabbing my wrist. "You took this too far — we need to go to the headmaster."

My eyes burn with anger. "They said they didn't want to do it anymore, that they wouldn't eat the sacrifice, that . . . it was a waste. But it's you who are the waste. All of *you*."

"You've lost your grip, Kitty. It's gone too far — you've gone too far." Wells begins to cry, weep, really, and I can't watch. He is not the man I thought he was.

I run into the woods, away from the girls I thought were my family, from the man I thought was my future.

Thinking I am alone, I let myself cry at the edge of the tree line, Glennmare in the distance. Exhausted, I lean against a tree, wondering if I really have lost it. Am I mad, crazed?

Everyone in the cabin looked at me with horror. Now, I don't know how I can ever return to them. I'm sobbing, exhausted, when I hear the footsteps.

It's a woman I have never seen before, with blue eyes as bright as the moon.

"Are you okay?" she asks. "There is blood on your gown."

I shake my head, disgusted. "I'm not hurt. Not physically. Emotionally?" I laugh tight and sharp. "The man I love just betrayed me. So in that regard, I have never felt less okay in my life."

"Do you need help? I can help you get back to the school. You're shaking."

I wipe my nose. "Who are you?"

"I'm Eleanor, I was just walking to my car. Do you need a ride?"

"A ride?"

She nods. "Sure, is there some place you want to go?"

"Just away from here, for one night."

"Sure," she says. "I can take you somewhere."

She offers me her coat, wraps it around my shoulders and I lean into her, feeling stunned by the betrayal in the cabin. In my dreams, it was going to feel a lot more ethereal. In reality, it felt cold, forced, nothing like how I imagined it.

My stomach turns and I vomit on the grass. "Sorry."

"It's okay. You seem worn out."

"I'm so tired," I tell her, getting in the passenger seat of her car. I close my eyes as she drives, unable to keep them open. When the car stops, I wake. "Where are we?"

"Whidbey Inn. I'm staying here. Want to come inside and get something to eat? Maybe a shower? You can use my phone."

"I don't have anyone to call," I mumble, following her out of the parking lot and down a path. "You're not in the main lodge?" I ask, relieved that someone is taking care of me. Tomorrow I'll go to Seattle and find a clinic to deal with the pregnancy.

"No, I have a cabin on the lagoon." She smiles warmly, and I decide to trust her because I have no one else.

Once inside the cozy cabin, I let my shoulders fall. "You mentioned a shower?"

She nods. "Sure, I'll show you the restroom. Actually, how does a bath sound? The water pressure is pretty terrible."

"Sure," I say, stepping into the bath water, still in my gown. She looks away, as if embarrassed, not realizing I am still dressed. I don't want to peel off the cloths of the night quite yet. I want to soak in the memories.

"You go to school at Glennmare?" she asks as I sink into the tub.

"Yeah, or at least I did. I think I'm ready for a change, though."

I know this woman is a stranger and that no one knows where I am — but I don't have room in my mind to care. All that matters right now is that I am away from my so-called friends and my weak lover. My mind is in knots, I need my medicine, and I am so, so tired.

"Just relax," Eleanor says, and I do. In the warmth, I let go of the night, of everything. I close my eyes and sink under the water, and I don't realize at first that Eleanor is leaning over me until it's too late. And she's pressing a towel over my mouth, and holding me down under the water.

I claw at the tub, at her, kicking and screaming, but my head stays submerged. I can't lift it, no matter what I do, and this woman is so much stronger that it's impossible to fight, though I try.

My head is empty, my mind numb, my life over.

CHAPTER 56. THE GIRLS

Four days ago, we went to a cabin to pretend to act in a performance of an ancient rite that will forever stain our memories. There was a sacrifice, and his name was Eli.

Since then, we have stayed awake at night, asking one another if we are to blame. We could have told the police, the teachers, Kitty's parents — told them everything. We didn't. We held our secrets close to our chests out of loyalty. Out of fear.

We wonder if we could have stopped things before they got too far. Were we responsible? Were we liable for what happened next?

We loved Wells because he was good to us, but, now, as we pace the dormitory, knowing tomorrow half of the school will leave, we wonder if he was ever good at all. To us or to Kitty. After Kitty went missing, we clung to Wells because we kept his secrets. Letting him go would mean the memories were ours alone.

Kitty was easy to love because she made life at Glennmare feel like a fairy tale, like a web she spun, that we were caught in. Being in her orbit made life feel bigger, better, ours.

All we know is that after the pair left the cabin four days ago, we were abandoned, and all we had was one another. We didn't want to get the people we loved in any more trouble. Besides, we knew we were also to blame.

We remembered the abandoned well that was covered with a piece of plywood and rocks, next to the cabin. We looked at one another, horrified with what we needed to do, but made the decision nonetheless.

We used the machete. We are not proud. We cried silent tears, unable to speak as we made Eli, who had been a living, breathing man, small enough to move. It is shocking the things you will do when you love someone. We were willing to clean up Kitty's mess, even if it meant the blood was on our hands.

The four of us took corners of the tarp and tugged, pulling until we were breathless, bearing down with our weight as we pulled pieces of the fallen man out through the cabin door. Bernie shouted, Diane wept, Jolie directed, Coretta was shocked silent. We moved the plywood and rocks aside, the well shadowy and deep and three feet wide.

We were covered in the blood of a man we didn't even know, a sacrifice for a rite we never wanted to understand, the baby in Kitty's belly not even Wells'.

Was any of our time with Kitty real?

And what did it mean, the fact we still loved her with all our hearts? She hurt us and we would still do anything to protect her.

What Kitty did in the cabin was not the Kitty we knew.

We could separate the two. *We had to.*

The Kitty who pulled the trigger on that gun was a ghost of the one we whispered with in our dorm at night. Not the same Kitty who baked us birthday cakes and wrote us lines of poetry, tucking the papers into our hands as we walked the halls of Glennmare.

We believed we were wise and strong because we knew that Kitty was not herself that night in the cabin with the Knight's Rite on her mind. And so, we wouldn't tell anyone what she did. It wouldn't be fair to victimize the Kitty who loved us because of the Kitty we never knew.

But now, on the eve of so many girls leaving for home, after the headmaster's scandal and Johanna's suicide, the four of us are called, as a group, to the library. Our hearts pound as we enter the same room where, earlier in the afternoon, we spoke with our parents.

Now, there is a man we don't recognize — probably the interim headmaster — and a police officer. Not the detectives, though — someone else. She is older, with graying hair and lips pressed tightly together.

"I am the police chief, Janice Richards," she says. "I am aware you four are the closest students to Katherine Calloway?"

Coretta clears her throat. "Yes. We're her roommates. Did you find her?"

Chief Richards looks at the man, then back at us. "Yes, we did find her. However, I am so sorry to tell you, we found her body. Miss Calloway passed away."

"What?" Diane shakes her head. "When?"

"According to our estimation, it was late Friday night," the chief tells us.

"How?" Bernie asks.

The chief looks down, not wanting to meet our eyes. "It appears she drowned."

"Drowned?" Jolie swallows. "Where?"

"In a bathtub, in a hotel in Whidbey," the woman explains. "Unfortunately, I do not have more information at this time. However, her parents did request we let you know about your friend."

"Oh my God." Diane begins to sob, clutching us, and we hold her, hold one another. So much death in one night.

"I know it has been a long, eventful day," the man says, not having introduced himself. "You are free to stay down here as long as you like or return to your rooms. I am aware that some of you are leaving tomorrow morning."

"Thank you for telling us," Coretta says.

We leave together, up the grand staircase to our room, where we collapse.

After everything . . . she's really gone.

"Is it our fault?" Diane whispers. "If we had just gone along with what she wanted, she wouldn't have gotten mad and left the cabin and . . . she would still be here."

"Could you have done it?" Jolie asks. "I couldn't stomach any more."

"Do you think Wells will ever remember?" Coretta asks.

For the last few days, it was all we wanted — for him to remember so we could have answers about what happened when the two of them left the cabin. When they left us to clean up the mess, to dispose of the dead man, to rid the cabin of the cauldron, the fire pit, to set Lily free, everything. We buried the sacrifice in the well with tear-streaked eyes and hands shaking and hearts ripped out. If he remembered, it would mean we could find our fragile friend.

Now, we know where Kitty is, and there is no need for any of us to remember the night. It needs to be blasted from our minds, forever.

A chill rolls around the room. "For his sake, I hope he never does," Jolie says.

CHAPTER 57. WELLS

I watched as Kitty left me, sobbing as she ran through the woods, back to the academy. I took the black horse from where it was tied to the tree and mounted it, forcing myself to separate this animal from the white mare. If I compartmentalized the night I could move on. Maybe I shouldn't have had the chance.

My entire body was racked with horror. How did I stand by while she killed a man?

What sort of man was I?

I desired a girl who was barely a woman, stood by as she shot someone. Let her run away into the woods instead of grabbing her wrist and forcing her to go to the police.

The only thing any of that said about me was that I was weak.

On the horse, riding toward the shore, I made a choice. It was the only move I had. I would swim out to sea and let myself be taken by the frigid waters, the desolate ocean. I would let myself sink to the floor, where my body could decompose. I would go where I belonged — to hell.

As I reached the shore, I saw a woman nearing me. Calling for me. No. I needed to do this now, and I didn't want anyone to stop me.

"I know it was you," the woman shouted. "I know you did this to her. She is just a child!"

"A child? Who are you?" But then I pulled back on the reins as she came into view, the light of the moon shining down on her face.

Johanna.

"She told me she was pregnant, and I put two and two together — you are always with her." The cook lifted her arm, and I couldn't tell what she held, but a moment later I felt it. She'd thrown a large rock straight at my head. It hit my arm, and I winced in shock.

Stunned, I pulled on the reins, wanting to turn the stallion around, but the horse was afraid and spooking at the commotion and began to pick up speed, running down the shore where trees overhung the beach.

"Stop," I yelled, trying to calm the horse. "Slow down. I got you."

In my gut I believed he knew what I had done and decided to make me pay.

He began to gallop, full on.

A rock was the least of my concern. Now, I was about to collide with a large branch, and while I could hold on to the reins to avoid more injury — I chose, instead, to let go.

I deserved to die. I wanted to.

Falling from the horse, my foot caught in the stirrup, my body began to bounce as I was dragged over the rocks, until I finally broke free. My body smashing against a rock, for the final blow. Then everything went black.

CHAPTER 58. DETECTIVE LEONARD ABBOTT

At the station, Tippy Brimble sits behind a metal desk in a plastic chair. She is a petite woman with a nice haircut and bright eyes. But behind all that, I know there is something sinister.

Phoebe sits beside me; the video and audio recordings are on, and we are poised with lukewarm coffee, pens and paper.

Tippy's hands shake, and she laces her fingers, as if praying this isn't happening.

But it is. It's time she answers our questions.

"We found Katherine Calloway's body in the cabin you've been renting for two weeks. How did she arrive there?"

She is shaking, she is exhausted. We can use that to our advantage.

"I don't know how you knew it was me. I paid in cash, I used an alias, I . . ."

"The island isn't very big, Ms. Brimble. Eventually there's always a crack."

"And the crack is Freddy. That is why you came asking for him tonight, wasn't it? He knew something." She shakes her head, bewildered. As if she truly thought her privilege would keep her from fault.

But she is wrong about Frederick. When we came to the door of Wells' cottage, we didn't know she was to blame.

"I . . . I . . ." She begins to cry, but her tears are worthless in this room. "She came in my car. I drove her there . . . she fell asleep in the bath and . . . I didn't know what to do."

"So you left her there?" Phoebe asks. "After she drowned? When you knew we were looking for her. You pretended for four days you had never heard of the girl?"

"I didn't know what to do . . . I was stuck. Wells needed help and so I just focused on him."

"And pretended there wasn't a dead girl in the bathtub?"

She wrings her hands. "I know, it's bad, I just, I wanted to help Wells and I knew I couldn't if people knew Katherine was in my cabin. I would be . . . I wouldn't be able to help him. And that's all I wanted. To help my friend. That's why I tried to start the fire at the cabin tonight. I wanted to protect him from those girls, get him away from them."

"Did you know Katherine before Friday night, when you brought her to your lodgings?"

"Knew *of* her."

"How?" I ask.

"I had seen her, I mean. I had, I knew she loved Wells and . . ." She shakes her head. "I'm sorry, can I get a lawyer?"

"We already told you that was your right."

She begins to cry harder. "I didn't think this would be so hard. So . . ."

"Incriminating?" Phoebe asks coldly.

Tippy looks at us, her eyes full of the realization of just how much trouble she is in. "Don't just look at me! It's Wells' fault. He's the reason I pushed her under the water! I wanted her dead. He's . . . he's . . ."

There. A confession. And she is so out of her element she doesn't even realize the words she's said.

"What?" Phoebe asks. "What is he?"

Her face falls, her shoulders go slack, she slumps in the chair. "The man I love?"

"Why were you staying at the inn?" I ask. "Frederick was under the impression you had been in Oregon."

"I came here because I was in love with Wells, only he hated me because of what happened last summer. I thought I could see what his life was like, see how I might get a second chance with him. I never imagined he would be obsessed with a bunch of teenagers."

"So you had been following him?" Phoebe asks.

Tippy scoffs. "Don't make me out to be some crazed stalker. I was watching to see if he was okay. He had cut me out of his life, he'd cut out Freddy. Clearly, he needed an intervention. He thought he was in love with that child!"

"We found these in Wells' cottage. Can you tell me about them?" I pull out the cards from the evidence bag, found in a box in the hallway, along with a machete, a lock of hair, and a few notes.

"After she . . . died . . . I went to the cabin to find Wells, but I couldn't find him anywhere. The girls were outside, freaking out, so I went inside the cabin and took a few things. The girls were panicking, and must have thought everything was thrown into the well. And yes, the gun used to kill that man was tossed in with his body, but these things were salvaged by me."

"What other things did you take?"

"The knife. The cards. Just those two things."

"And you put them in Wells' cottage?"

She nods numbly. "While he slept, I added them to the other things I found in his house — the notes and lock of hair, this was before Freddy got there."

"Why would you put incriminating evidence back in Wells' home if you loved him?" I ask.

"When I took the stuff from the barn, I never imagined Kitty would die or that Wells would lose his memory. I only brought this stuff out and showed him and Freddy when I realized nothing was stopping Wells from getting close to the girls. Even with Kitty dead, with me setting fire to the cabin — none of it was going to stop him from wanting them more than me."

"Did Freddy know about any of this?"

Tippy squeezes her eyes shut, as if conceding. "No, Freddy knew nothing."

"And the cards, what are these?"

Tippy barks out an exhausted laugh. "That is what they wanted to do in the cabin Friday night. Check the well and you'll find the sacrifice."

My jaw clenches. These cards depict inhuman acts of horror. "All of this?"

She nods. "Well, not exactly. Instead of the horse, she sacrificed a man. Katherine was the freakish ringleader." She points to the man and horse, together. My stomach rolls. "They weren't going to go along with the plan until Katherine took the gun out . . . and that weirdo Eli was so busy stalking Kitty he didn't see it coming."

"Eli?" I ask.

Tippy nods. "Some guy here on the island camping, from what I could tell, obsessed with Kitty and always watching her from a distance. He was there, at the cabin that night, and Kitty heard him outside, dragged him into the cabin."

I look at Baker, realizing we overlooked a potential link between the missing man who had been camping and Katherine. "The missing camper. You know where he is?"

Tippy nods. "Well, let's just say he's gone. The girls took care of his body after Kitty and Wells ran off."

Phoebe grips the edge of the table, and for a moment I think she may faint. She's one of the toughest people I know.

"Insane, right?" Tippy says. "But it's true, I saw them through the cracks in the cabin wall. They chopped that man up and dropped him in the well."

"And Halifax, what is his part in all of this?" I ask her.

She shakes her head slowly. Her shoulders rise then fall, as if she is all out of air, the reality of the situation finally hitting home. "You should talk to Wells yourself. After all, now he can remember."

* * *

After detaining Tippy and keeping her in custody for what will undoubtedly be an impending sentencing, Phoebe and I walk outside to take a breather. Wells Halifax is in a holding cell, but the conversation we need to have with him is going to require us to be fully alert. It can wait until tomorrow.

"Unbelievable," I say, shaking my head. "I always knew that academy was fucked up, but this? This is next level."

"Tippy is a sociopath. Leaving that poor girl dead, for days . . ." Phoebe presses her hands to her temples. "Leo, I don't know if I'll get over it."

"Those girls must be traumatized."

"Not to mention they are accessories to murder," I say, trying to register everything we just learned from Tippy. "The blood on Kitty's dress must have been from Eli ... she was a murderer before she was murdered."

To say it was shocking is an understatement. I look up at the blue sky clouds have been lifted from so much, it seems. Still, there is plenty of darkness lurking in this case.

The girls, according to Tippy, dismembered and concealed the body of Eli.

"A lawyer will get them off of that charge, they were being emotionally manipulated," Phoebe says.

"I think so too. The part that is most wild is the fact that Tippy learned that Kitty was not in fact pregnant by Wells. I assumed the worst with that man."

"He was still a creep, even if he wasn't sleeping with his students. He crossed lines. I hope he never gets the chance to teach again."

"We might never have the truth, but I wonder if Tippy was doubly motivated to kill Kitty once she learned that she lied about Wells being the father."

Phoebe presses her lips together, considering that. "Tippy's obsession with protecting Wells was beyond comprehension. I wouldn't doubt this motive."

The horror of it all is lodged in my throat and I feel like I could cry . . . imagining Cassidy losing her life over a grown woman's jealousy is unfathomable. "To kill a child . . . and her unborn child . . . it's incomprehensible."

There are tears in her eyes. "No one ever wants to imagine the world could be this messed up, but it is. Makes me lose my faith in humanity, you know?"

I wrap an arm around her shoulder. "Hey, chin up. Even with all that bad out there, there is an awful lot of good."

She looks up at me. "Cassidy's lucky to have a dad like you."

Somehow, despite the day, I smile. "Speaking of, I need to get home to her. We need rest. It's been one hell of a day."

Phoebe yawns, proving my point. "Good thing Frederick came to the island."

"I'm glad he went with his instincts, even though it meant his sister was incriminated."

"*Step*sister," Phoebe clarifies.

"Is there a reason for the distinction?"

Phoebe looks at me like I've lost it. "Freddy and Tippy were sleeping together."

I scratch my head. "How do you know that?"

She groans. "The writing was on the wall from the first conversation we had with them. That trio was all too twisted for anything good to come of it."

I shake my head. "Could it get any worse?"

Phoebe looks off in the distance. "All I know is there are a bunch of girls who really need to get home."

CHAPTER 59. FREDDY

Tippy didn't make bail, and for that I am glad. Wells is still being detained. My father and stepmother are flying in this evening and eventually they will know the entirety of the situation. While I am not exactly looking forward to the moment that they realize Tippy and I slept together . . . I am done with secrets. They never suited me much anyways.

Lighting a cigarette as I walk through town, it's obvious my time here on this wind-blown island is ending. I won't be staying past tomorrow.

"Freddy." Marjorie brings me to the present moment — the frosty February morning and the water shimmering on the horizon, as if inviting me on an adventure. Bumping into her on the sidewalk somehow feels like a comfort.

"Hello, Marjorie." I smile warmly, stubbing out my cigarette, wafting my hand through the air to clear it, pleased to see the tarot reader who propelled me toward buying a boat and following my buried dream. "I suppose you've heard?"

"Everyone on the island has." She shakes her head. "Have you eaten? I was just headed to Whidbey Coffee Company. Join me?"

"I'd love to." I turn with her toward the local café.

Once seated with cappuccinos and pastries, Marjorie leans in across the table. "I heard you were the one who found Katherine Calloway."

Letting out an exhale, I nod. "With Dale, who works at the Whidbey Inn."

"He's the one who told me. Poor guy seemed so distraught about the whole thing."

"I'd never seen a dead body before and would have preferred things stayed that way."

She exhales, breaking a sugar-glazed donut in two. "Dale also said he was helping you secure a boat. You're leasing one of his?"

"Yes, finally my youth spent at summer sailing camps will be put to use."

She smiles. "I take it you have embraced your fortune after all."

"What do you mean?"

"The Knight of Pentacles. Choosing a path and working toward that destination. You will do good, Frederick. But make no mistake, it will require constant and steady work. And according to the card, over time there will be slow and steady financial improvement."

"Considering I told my father I no longer wanted his money and will need to rely on my own ingenuity from here forward, that better come true."

Marjorie's eyes widen in surprise. "You cut ties with your mogul parents? I am thoroughly impressed."

I shrug, biting into my apple Danish. "I need to be my own man."

She twists her lips, looking at me. "And you thought the card was meant for Wells Halifax."

A chill runs up my spine. "That was before I learned my dearest friend was so weak."

"I don't know about all that," she says gently.

I clench my jaw, wishing I didn't know either.

"Once the case goes to trial, everyone can weigh in on what they think his culpability is in all this."

"Do you need to stick around for that?" Marjorie asks.

"I'm leaving for a bit, headed out on the open water. But I will be called in as a witness in the trial since I am the one who discovered Katherine's body." I shake my head, wishing it was over already. "Hopefully it won't take long before I can put this behind me."

Marjorie finishes her latte. "Want a word of advice?"

I chuckle. "At this point, I feel inclined to do anything you say."

She bites her bottom lip, thinking. "Thing is, people are going to keep disappointing you, lying to you, cheating you — all your life. And sure, we can keep pulling cards to seal our fate. But I prefer to pull up my bootstraps."

I lift my eyebrows. "You do remember you're a tarot-card reader?"

"The thing is, the cards were never meant to choose our fate. They are there to help us see our potential. But deep down, we most often already know what we truly desire, what we wish for in life."

"Do you still remember: falling stars, how they leapt slantwise through the sky, like horses over suddenly held-out hurdles of our wishes?" I quote the poet Rilke.

I think back to the steps outside the building at Yale, all those years ago. The night air, the way Tippy's beret sat crooked on her head. Wells and his hand-rolled cigarettes, his rumpled suit. Me, with my heart on my sleeve, wanting to be more than I was.

Marjorie smiles widely at me, quoting Rilke right back. "Our wishes — did we have so many? — for stars, innumerable, leapt everywhere."

I break into a grin. This tarot reader from the other side of the world, in her sneakers and polar-fleece vest, is more kindred to me than I would have believed possible.

Memories of Wells and Tippy quoting Whitman that first night we met come to me now. Whitman said the answers would be found within us, in our choices and how we contribute. But that doesn't mean the night sky isn't still filled with stars.

And when I look up, I can see there are many wishes within me still, waiting to be fulfilled.

I can start my life again, without false bravado or grandeur.

Simply put, I can live.

CHAPTER 60. THE GIRLS

Saying goodbye is horrendous. Tears streak our cheeks, our hearts, our souls. Parting feels impossible, but bags are packed and planes are landing and boats are leaving. Our parents have all hired teams of lawyers to protect us. Finally, they are willing to step in on our behalf. Why did it have to take Kitty dying for them to care?

It's not a question we will ever have an answer to.

Our time at Glennmare will never escape us. Journalists will make sure of that.

We are not blameless, sure. The things we did that night in the cabin will become our crosses to bear. We watched a man die, then we used a machete to get rid of him.

We will not pretend otherwise. When the story breaks, and it eventually will, we will be cast as characters. We won't be seen as real.

After all, we are just girls.

Girls who must have asked for it.

Girls who can't be trusted, anyway.

Girls who are not victims, surely. They walked into the cabin of their own accord!

Girls who could have spoken up sooner.

Girls who chose to stay silent.

Girls who.

Girls.

Girls who kiss goodbye on the green lawn of Glennmare, our white dresses billowing around us, buoying our broken hearts.

Girls who make promises for a future that is both blindingly bright and inescapably narrow.

Girls who want it all but are not sure how to get there.

Girls who whisper, "We will get there, together."

THE END

THE JOFFE BOOKS STORY

We began in 2014 when Jasper agreed to publish his mum's much-rejected romance novel and it became a bestseller.

Since then we've grown into the largest independent publisher in the UK. We're extremely proud to publish some of the very best writers in the world, including Joy Ellis, Faith Martin, Caro Ramsay, Helen Forrester, Simon Brett and Robert Goddard. Everyone at Joffe Books loves reading and we never forget that it all begins with the magic of an author telling a story.

We are proud to publish talented first-time authors, as well as established writers whose books we love introducing to a new generation of readers.

We have been shortlisted for Independent Publisher of the Year at the British Book Awards three times, in 2020, 2021 and 2022, and for the Diversity and Inclusivity Award at the Independent Publishing Awards in 2022.

We built this company with your help, and we love to hear from you, so please email us about absolutely anything bookish at feedback@joffebooks.com.

If you want to receive free books every Friday and hear about all our new releases, join our mailing list: www.joffebooks.com/contact.

And when you tell your friends about us, just remember: it's pronounced Joffe as in coffee or toffee!

Milton Keynes UK
Ingram Content Group UK Ltd.
UKHW011825041223
433774UK00002B/7

9 781835 263075